I0772597

ICE BORN

ICE BORN

ADAM FERNANDEZ

Clover Hill Press
New Jersey

"We fight, we fall, our tales are told."

Armanic Proverb

CHAPTER

1

"Hey, Cap? Can you wait a minute?"

Henry stopped and turned. "What is it, Sergeant?"

Arabella waited until the rest of their party stepped further down the busy street. She wanted privacy. "I need to make a stop."

He looked like he had been expecting something like this all along. He clenched his jaw, and his boyish face hardened. It reminded her of the first time they met, what felt like so long ago now on Mars.

"I thought you'd never been to the Saturnalian system before?" he said after a long moment.

She kept her expression neutral. "Visiting someone for a friend."

Henry looked concerned but didn't argue with her. She knew he wouldn't. They were both used to keeping secrets. "Try to keep it brief. I don't think Jimmy wants to stay here longer than we need to."

She nodded and turned to leave. It had been a long trip, and she was anxious to get this over with.

He reached out, grabbing her arm gently. "I can go with you if you like."

Arabella hesitated.

Her body wanted to say yes, but her mind knew this wasn't a visit he could make with her. On the long journey from Luna, they shared the surface of their collective scars. He asked about the stories written in ink on her skin, and she silently read the stories written in scars on his.

She put a hand on his cheek, holding it gently.

He leaned in and kissed her, the bustling neighborhood and the war they were fighting forgotten. Their companions, out of sight and out of mind. She pulled away reluctantly.

"I hope you don't intend to leave us, me," he said, looking at her seriously.

"This is no more my home than Mars or Luna. My place is wherever I choose to be."

He smiled, and she realized her mask had slipped. Meeting a man a decade younger, raised in a noble palace with scars deeper than her own had strained her commitment to her adopted persona. "Don't worry, Cap. I'll be back soon."

The others in their party had come back to look for them. Henry gave them a reassuring wave. "Okay, Sergeant. We shouldn't be far. Jimmy said he knew a place where we could keep a low profile. It's called Huygens Tavern."

She nodded. "I've heard of it. I'll be along as soon as I'm done."

Henry smirked. "Of course you have. You know a lot for someone who's never been here." His expression became more serious as he eyed passersby warily. "Call if you need me, and I'll come running."

"I know." She returned his smile and continued toward her true destination. She didn't look back to see if he lingered.

The crowds here didn't bother her, in part because they separated as she approached. The Armanic tattoos on her face and the reputation they carried would make the petty criminals wary enough not to cross her. The pistol on her hip would discourage the rest.

Only soldiers carried guns openly within the Republic. That might change in time with the onset of the revolution, but it wouldn't be overnight. The revolution was still a faraway notion to the people of the Far Coast, the moons and planets beyond the asteroid belt.

The conflict on the Neptunian moon Triton was closer to home for them but still a lifetime away for people who rarely left their own neighborhoods. Arabella was amazed by how many more had no idea about either conflict. News was traveling very slowly and being skillfully suppressed by the Republic's secret police, the Frumentarii, and other loyalist elements.

She turned down a smaller alley off the main corridor. Here the shop stalls extended out into the roadway limiting traffic to only small vehicles, mainly hoverbikes or rickety wheeled motorbikes. Henry might have been uneasy in this neighborhood, but it was far from the worst parts of town. More of a working-class mid district than anything resembling a slum.

Shopkeepers shouted their specials at her as she walked. They were excited by the prospect of a visitor with a military paycheck to spend. They held up scarves and other clothing, hand-crafted trinkets, and all manner of half-broken tech devices.

Then there was the food. Rice dishes mixed with vegetables and unidentifiable meat. All made on street carts of dubious quality by people with even more questionable hygiene. The food carried a familiar aroma that momentarily warmed her soul. Until the same smells threatened to dredge up the memories she had buried away.

Normally she would have dismissed those rumblings and focused on the task at hand. That wouldn't work now because her task was as much about her memories as anything else. She had unfinished business that fate had given her a chance to rectify. It was a long time coming, and she was determined not to waste the opportunity.

Arabella found the business she was looking for. It was in a dirty alley several streets down from an abandoned spaceport. The district no longer manufactured much and therefore had little use for a facility dedicated to the import of raw materials. When the jobs vanished, so did the people. They left to find brighter prospects elsewhere, leaving the spaceport an anachronistic relic of better times.

The windows on the front of the establishment were blacked out. Only a small neon sign that flickered sadly suggested it was occupied at all. The sign was missing several letters, but she knew what it once said, "Finns's Bar and Hostel." She remembered it as a bustling hub of the neighborhood. Now it was the kind of place strangers wouldn't visit.

Arabella opened the creaky door and was immediately struck by a blast of stale air from inside. The lights were dim, and a layer of dust clung to everything. She thought for a moment she was wrong and the bar was abandoned years ago.

Until a man stirred in his chair beside the door like an awakened mummy. His eyes were heavy as if she awoke him from a centuries-long slumber. He eyed her suspiciously, a hand moving toward a cudgel on his hip.

Another pale-skinned apparition appeared behind the bar. Like a caricature of a bartender, he stood drying a glass with a dirty rag. The bar was long and held seats for nearly a dozen, but only one at the very end was filled. The man in it was quite fat, and she commended the resolve of the old stool he sat on to remain steadfast in its unenviable duty.

Arabella approached the bar, unconcerned with the man by the door or at the end of the bar. "Beer," she said, looking the bartender up and down.

He was shorter than she remembered. His face had the appearance of bleached leather, which made him look much older than the fifty-some-odd years he was. He was a fellow Armanic but bore no tattoos. A sign his life lacked any accomplishments their people deemed worth celebrating.

The bartender waved, and she heard the guard return to his seat behind her. "We don't get many visitors through here these days." She assumed that was his way of explaining the rudeness. He didn't recognize her, but that was for the best.

"I'm here on business," she said, not trying to hide her Lunese accent. "Where's the boss?"

He placed a glass of what passed for beer in this dump in front of her. "And who are you?"

Hearing the question, the fat man at the end of the bar got up to approach her, his stool creaking in relief. He was dark skinned and wore a scarf in the Mercurian style around his head.

"Boss isn't expecting any visitors. Why don't you piss off."

Arabella downed her drink, and the bartender tensed. The liquid was sour and burned her throat, but she found it oddly comforting in its familiarity. "Do I look like I give a shit what he's expecting?"

"You seem like a smart woman. Don't go chasing trouble, stranger. This isn't the place," the bartender said.

The scarfed man stepped closer. He was several inches shorter than her, but his prodigious belly easily filled the space between them. He was trying to make it harder for her to draw her pistol.

"Who gives a shit what you want? The Jeevan on your face means sarding nothing to me. I won't tell ya again." His breath stank of cheap liquor, and he flashed a lightning cudgel at his waist.

Arabella casually retrieved a case of cigarettes from the inside pocket of her jacket, revealing the Republican Guard insignia on her uniform in the process.

The large man took a step back as if he saw a snake. "We already squared up with the Resident Watch."

Moving slowly, deliberately, she took a cigarette from the case and placed it on her lips. Lighting it, she returned the case to her pocket. "I care even less about those pissants. I said I'm here to see the boss."

"Sorry, ma'am, if you would have identified yerself, there wouldn't have been any trouble from us," the bartender offered diplomatically, and the large man hurried to agree.

"Are you going to take me to him or not?" she said, impatiently.

The large man stumbled, knocking over a stool in his haste to lead the way.

Before following him, she pulled out a credit chip far larger than the drink deserved and tossed it to the bartender. "Keep the change."

She always liked Finn, despite everything that had happened. Arabella knew he wasn't the one to blame. She gave him a small wink, and for a moment there was a flash of familiarity in his eyes.

Did I let too much slip too soon?

Then the look passed, and she relaxed. She needed to be more careful. What were a few more minutes after so many years of waiting.

Arabella was led down a short hallway leading to a series of rooms in the rear of the building. Past a staircase that led up to a collection of small guest rooms. There was a chain blocking the dusty stairs, so she assumed the rooms must be empty. She couldn't imagine who would pay to stay here by choice in its current state.

The walls were filthy, and the once brightly colored wallpaper was torn or rotten. She ran a finger over an old bullet hole that graced the wall beside her, her mind briefly going somewhere else. They never even bothered patching it.

At the end of the hallway was another guard sitting in front of a door that led to a small apartment. His skin was rough and heavily pockmarked, but he looked more capable then the others. When they approached, he rose from his chair, hefting a rail rifle.

Arabella adjusted her stance and prepared to use the fat man as a shield and battering ram if it came to it. It turned out to be unnecessary.

The fat man shouted, "Got a guardsman here to see the boss."

The rifleman grunted and ducked inside. He returned a moment later to wave her in. Arabella took the last drag of her cigarette and put it out on the door frame before entering.

The room had a stale odor of nectar smoke and sickness that clung to everything. It hadn't been what she was expecting, but at least the smoke from nectar was less debilitating than the injected form of the drug. She didn't come here to speak with a drug-addled mess.

The two guards followed her in and motioned to a pair of empty chairs. Beside the table was a game board for playing Go. Black and white stones sat in separate bowls beside the board.

The rest of the room was cluttered with numerous shelves holding all manner of trinkets and baubles. The space looked more like a curio shop than an office. On the opposite end of the room from where she entered was another door that led into the adjoining living space.

She wasn't surprised he would make her wait. The Mizraei she knew seemed to like a bit of the dramatic. She paid no attention to the guard with the gun who watched her anxiously, a local street tough by the look of him.

Instead, she studied the fat man. Not because he was Mercurian but because she remembered his part in this too. When she finished with Mizraei, she would settle up with him too.

The wait was longer than she expected, the day continuing to go against her expectations. It was perhaps an omen she chose to ignore. Fate had its own rules, and she didn't claim to understand them.

When Pakur Mizraei finally emerged from his bedroom, she could see why it took so long. He shambled out like a corpse, his cane rapping on the ground signaling his frailty. While his cloudy eyes made her wonder if he could even see her at all. His once colorful robes were faded and looked several sizes too big. The image she had lived with all these years was a distant memory.

The rifleman rushed over to lead Mizraei by the arm to one of the empty chairs.

Maybe it was all for show, she thought, taking the other seat.

"My man tells me the Republican Guard has come to pay me a visit." Mizraei looked past her as he fell heavily into the chair. His tan skin looked sickly and hung loosely over his once-muscular build.

"Sergeant Smith, I'm here to ask you a few questions," she said formally. "Alone."

Neither guard moved until Mizraei said, "Go, I've no fear of Republic henchmen, but I do wonder why you're here. The great Mizraei is retired, so you'll have to find another business partner for whatever scheme you're involved in."

The guards left, closing the door behind them, although Arabella could still hear the fat man's heavy breathing through the thin wall.

She tried to ignore the acrid smell of nectar smoke that clung to Mizraei. "We're investigating Coalition cells in the region. You're well connected, aren't you?"

"Maybe once," he said, pulling a pipe out of a pocket. "Like I said, I'm retired."

"Strange a Mercurian of means like yourself stayed here to retire. So far away from the warmth."

"Is it any stranger than a Lunese Armanic with a Jeevan on her face in my home? I haven't seen Mercury in sixty years. By that metric I wager I'm less a Solite than you are."

The term Solite was mainly used by Armanics of the Far Coast to describe those with heritage originating from the Inner Solar System. It was usually used pejoratively.

Mizraei's cloudy eyes dug into her, struggling to make out the details of her face. She worried he would figure out who she was. She wanted answers before that happened.

"Do you stay here because the Coalition wants you too?" She had to steer the topic away from herself.

He laughed. "I have no affiliation with those misfits. The Great Mizraei works for himself, and those who pay him of course." A hint of his youthful bravado shone through the malaise. He had a reputation as a great smuggler once, long ago.

"Are you saying the Coalition is the highest bidder these days?"

"I'd not tie myself to that rotten lot," he said dismissively. "Never worked with them before, not starting now. If someone told you otherwise, you have bad information."

She assumed that was a lie. "Okay, then why don't you tell me how you came to own this shit hole?"

"You can check the official records," he said, taking a puff of his pipe. "But I bought it along with the spaceport after finishing a big job. I wanted a stable home for my shipping business and to settle down after years of wandering. The Coalition and their meddling mucked it up for me though. Now no one comes here at all. Half the city is empty, and shipping traffic is being heavily diverted elsewhere."

"You mean you were going to use the spaceport to hide your smuggling operations?" she said, reading between the lines.

"Are you sure you aren't with the Frumentarii?" he said, eyeing her again. "Never met a guardsman who cared this much about business. You can check my books. They're all legitimate."

"I'm sure," she said dryly, "but I'm not an accountant. The Republican Guard is searching for the source of weapons and military equipment being moved by the Coalition from the Far Coast to the Inner System."

"You came to the wrong place," he said, looking off at the curios on his shelves. She got the sense that he was being honest. In his disinterest in their conversation, he stared into the distance.

She followed his eyes to a large pink gemstone in one of the glass cases. Her heart skipped a beat in recognition. It was a beautiful stone. Much too beautiful for this godforsaken place.

"That is for me to decide," she said firmly. "What's your association with the Serras?" On the surface, it should have been an innocuous question, but she fought to keep her voice and demeanor neutral.

He turned back sharply. "The Lords of Jupiter? None. Do I look like a sarding lord or magnate to you? I'm certainly no cleric."

"You're the great Pakur Mizraei, aren't you? The greatest smuggler in the Far Coast. Surely, they might have need of someone with your ability and connections to arrange the types of things they can't deal in personally."

He scoffed, "I'm only a merchant. Save your flattery for younger, more ambitious men."

"You didn't answer my question. I'm curious why it unsettled you so much." She leaned forward, jostling the table between them. The Go stones rattled in their wooden bowls. "What's your association with the Serras, old man."

Pakur leaned away from her aggression. He adjusted the jostled game board from a distance. "You'll need to be more specific. The Serras are numerous like weeds. I've dealt with some of them a time or two, like I've had dealings with various bishops of Saturn and a dozen other places. The great Mizraei is known far and wide in the realm of exotic and valuable goods."

Arabella steadied her breathing. "Why don't you start with the most recent dealing you've had with any of them? You don't want me to have to take you in as a relic dealer, do you? Or maybe an Imperialist sympathizer?"

He barely blinked at her threat. Instead, he motioned to the board. "Here, play a game with me."

"I didn't come here to steal money from a sarding blind man. I want information."

"Mizraei can see well enough for this. Humor an old man." He took another deep drag from his pipe. "First, you can tell me a story, and then I'll give you one in trade. A fair bargain among equals. You wear a Jeevan on your face. That's at least one story that demands telling."

"You're not my equal, and my business is my own."

He shrugged. "Then I have nothing else to say."

Arabella tried to control her frustration. "This will be easier if you cooperate."

"Look at me. A piece of fruit left to rot on the ground. No purpose and no value except to feed the worms. Nothing you do will change that, except speed along the inevitable. All I have now are stories to entertain me in the time I have left."

His lips curled into a sickly smile. "But I'm still a businessman. I'll answer your questions, but a story is my price." He raised a single, boney finger. "A real story that is." His cloudy eyes were digging into her, and she wondered what he saw.

Arabella took a deep breath and reached for her cigarette case. She hadn't smoked this much in years, but it helped to calm her nerves. A nervous tick she developed in the army.

Her eyes darted to the blank Go board. The bowl of black stones sat nearest to her, meaning it was her move. She picked one up and placed it near one of the corners. "Fine, but it may not be a story you'll enjoy. Try not to die before I finish telling it."

Mizraei grinned as if he had already won and placed a white stone in the opposite corner of the board to match her. "I'll stave off God's angels as long as I can."

CHAPTER

2

Juliana

June, 4083 U.E.T. - Argyphia, Enceladus

"Juliana, sit up straight," the headmistress shouted.

"Yes, Mistress," she replied, adjusting her posture.

Juliana's mind was already outside the dome, even if her trip wasn't for several hours.

Schoolwork couldn't compare to the prospect of such a unique adventure. The problem was her classroom only had three other children in it, plus her little brother Oliver, leaving her with nowhere to hide her inattention.

There used to be two more kids, but they left the dome one day without any explanation. After that happened, the remaining children were combined into one classroom with the school's headmistress as their only remaining teacher.

They were all between the ages of five and ten, with Juliana being nearly the oldest. On reflection, she probably was the oldest now that Morgan was gone. Her brother had just turned five and was the youngest in the class.

Juliana hoped maybe the other kids left to live outside on the ice. Because if they were living outside the dome, then maybe she would see them again soon when she went to visit. She missed playing with Morgan most of all. He was her best friend.

The headmistress pointed to the digiscreen displaying a view of Mars from orbit. Its surface was obscured by clouds, but it was easy to see a diverse and varied landscape with vast oceans, dry plains, forests, and snowcapped mountains.

"Who can tell me what the capital of the Republic is?"

"New Olympia," Juliana said confidently. It was better to get back on the teacher's good side, even if the question was meant for one of the younger kids.

"Good, and can you point to it on the map?"

Juliana got up from her seat and shuffled to the digiscreen. She promptly pointed out the location on the flanks of Olympus Mons. The big mountain by the sea made the location easy to remember.

"Very good, now sit down."

Juliana went back to her seat.

"New Olympia is our capital, and it is where the Vox and Manus, the voice and hand of God in this mortal plane, reside," the teacher went on.

Juliana knew all this already and found it incredibly boring. "What about Earth and Luna, the garden of Eden?" she asked, hoping to change the subject to something more interesting.

"Those are even further away. They are dark and dangerous places, full of pirates and demons. Mars is the light of our solar system and the only world you need to concern yourself with."

The teacher's response left her even more curious about Luna and the destroyed Earth. "Father says he'll take us to see Luna one day when he finishes working here. He used to live there," she said excitedly.

The headmistress looked down her nose at her. Juliana felt like she had said the wrong thing. "You need to focus on learning history and scripture so you can attend the Sanctum on Mars and study to join the clergy. That's why I'm here. It's the only thing you need to be thinking about."

She didn't enjoy studying scripture and had no interest in becoming a cleric. All they did was wear funny robes and talk about nothing. It was always a struggle to stay awake during church.

"What if I want to be a soldier like Kasperi?" she asked defiantly. Her mind always came back to Kasperi, her father's bodyguard. They always told her she couldn't be a soldier, but there were lots of them around. Why couldn't she be one too?

"Kasperi was born on the ice to be a soldier. You were born in the dome. I was brought here to make sure all of you are smarter and more successful than you would have been outside on the ice. That means attending an ecclesiastical school and joining the clergy, preferably on Mars," the headmistress said.

"But I'm Armanic like him," she countered.

It looked like her teacher was struggling to come up with a suitable response when the alarm marking the end of the day rang out. The bell distracted Juliana from her argument, and her mind shifted back to the excitement of her upcoming adventure.

She shot up to leave with the others, but the headmistress motioned for her to stay. Juliana slumped back into her seat expectantly, sparing a quick glance at her brother who looked worriedly at her before leaving the room.

The headmistress's expression softened as she approached her. She was an old woman with brown hair and dark-tan skin. She told the class she was from Mercury. Arabella looked at her own pale skin, whiter than the snow and ice outside the dome. She imagined everyone from so close to the sun must look like her teacher.

"Juliana, you're a clever girl from a noble family. You could be a bishop one day if you want to be. Do you know how many billions of people wish they could be you? Why do you want to fight?" she said, sitting down beside her.

"I don't know. I just want to be like Kasperi," Juliana said truthfully. "I'm going outside today on the ice."

The corners of the headmistress's mouth drew downward. "The ice isn't a good place, Juliana. I know I've told you that before."

"My mother is from the ice. I want to go and be like her. Like Kasperi too. I want to see it with my own eyes and not through the dome or a digiscreen."

"That's only because you've never been out there. You've never seen the darkness that lives outside the dome. You won't understand until you're older, but the solar system is a big place. The Inner System is far away, and the sun shines infinitely brighter compared to here. You'll see one day how much nicer it is, and you won't want to be outside on the ice or even in this dome."

"Why do you want to be here?" she asked.

The headmistress pursed her lips, as if she hadn't expected the question. "I made a mistake, and you know how scripture teaches about absolution? That's why I'm here."

Juliana nodded, even though she didn't really understand. She wanted to be dismissed so she could go meet her father for their trip.

The headmistress smiled weakly. "Go, we can talk more tomorrow."

That was all Juliana needed to hear, but she paused before bolting out of the schoolhouse. "I'm glad you're our headmistress."

The woman's smile grew as she shooed Juliana away.

Outside, her brother Oliver was waiting for her.

"Did you get in trouble?" he asked.

"No, headmistress wanted to talk to me, I guess. Come on. We need to get back home before we miss it."

"I don't mind," Oliver said with a groan. He was several years younger and lacked the natural curiosity Juliana was known for around the dome. That didn't stop her from dragging him around as her unwitting conspirator anyway.

She grabbed him by the arm and forced him into a run, even though his little legs struggled to keep up.

They ran through the dome that made up the totality of everything they had ever known of the real world. In the dome they had artificial lights that simulated the brightness of the twenty-four-hour light cycle of Old Earth. The buildings inside the dome were small, plain metal structures. They were huddled together into small compounds for the dozen or so families that called it home.

Since the dome was relatively small, it only took them fifteen minutes to make it back to their house. It was behind a short fence and had several buildings arranged around a central courtyard. Her father, Lord Serra, and Kasperi stood in the center near a waiting transport. They were directing workers to move supplies from the warehouse and onto the ship.

"We made it!" she shouted, skidding to a stop in the gravel. She was out of breath.

Their father glared in reprimand and returned to what he was doing. She realized she shouldn't have interrupted him and waited quietly on the balls of her feet for him to finish.

Oliver ran off to the storage lockers, returning a moment later with a heavy scarf and jacket. He struggled to carry them as he walked back to where they were standing, dragging the coat through the dirt. She was surprised he managed to retrieve it at all.

Her father was a tall man. Not as tall as Kasperi but still bigger than most of the workers. He was skinny with a bald head and a clean-shaven face. Although his skin was darker than hers or Mother's, it was still pale.

As a Jovian lord, his family had roots in the Inner System, so he would be considered a Solite by most. More contemptuously, they would call him an Imperial, given his noble roots with the long-dead Solar Empire. However, being an Imperialist sympathizer was an easy way to get in big trouble. So it wasn't a term people used lightly.

What set Father apart most was his gold and silver jewelry. A pair of light chains connected a ring in his nose to a collection of loops in his ears. Juliana always thought it looked uncomfortable, and he was the only one she knew of in the dome who wore them.

They were a symbol of the power and authority of their noble house that held large dominions on the moons of Jupiter. Why she lived on the moons of Saturn, far away from the other Serras, she never understood.

When their father finally finished, he came over to speak to her and Oliver. "You will both stay with Kasperi. Do you understand?"

Juliana acknowledged her father with a nod. She jabbed her brother's side with an elbow when he didn't answer.

Oliver nodded and rubbed at his ribs.

"Use your words."

"Yes, Father," they said in unison.

Lord Serra nodded his approval, the chains rattling softly, and he left them under Kasperi's watchful eye.

Kasperi looked down at her, "Where is your scarf and overcoat?" He spoke in a deep voice that reminded Juliana of a giant. At least what she thought a giant might sound like. She had never actually seen one, but her friend Morgan said they lived out on the ice.

"You haven't got one either," she said.

"I've got mine!" Oliver announced.

"I have my exoarmor. It will be very cold on the ice, nothing like in here," Kasperi said, motioning to the inside of the sunny dome. "Bare skin can freeze in less than a minute, and sometimes you can never warm it up again. You don't want that, do you?"

Juliana scowled. "I have my exosuit too," she said, pulling on the sleeve of her thin armor-like outfit. The exosuit would protect her skin against radiation and other elements, while a detachable mask provided fresh oxygen.

Kasperi sighed heavily and kneeled to look her in the eyes. On the bare skin of his neck and face, he had complex geometric tattoos that she knew covered the rest of his body as well. Some of the shapes were recognizable as mountains, trees, and other objects, but most were abstract to her. She used to think the tattoos made him look scary. Now she knew Kasperi was actually very nice, if a bit grumpy.

"You know it's dangerous out on the ice. You need to protect your skin and stay warm," he said softly. "The thin suit is not enough. Your skin isn't used to the cold."

"I'm not scared."

He smiled. "I know you aren't, but we must do what your father commands. He is the lord here." Kasperi leaned to whisper in her ear, "Your brother isn't as brave and strong as you. Don't you want to show him how to be brave? To protect him?"

Juliana turned to Oliver. He was looking nervously at her. It wasn't cold inside the dome, but he was already wearing his overcoat and scarf. She could see the sweat beading on his forehead.

She turned back to Kasperi. "Okay, I'll wear it."

"Good," he said, putting a large but gentle hand on her shoulder. "When we get on the ice, take Oliver's hand and stay close to me. Don't leave my sight."

Juliana nodded and walked over to Oliver. She yanked the scarf loose from around his neck and loosened the overcoat. "You don't need that yet."

He laughed nervously, "Thanks, it was really hot."

Juliana went to the storage room where they kept equipment like exosuits and outdoor tools. She retrieved an overcoat, scarf, and heavy mittens from the labelled cabinet. They had been trained in how to wear them in case of emergency, but she never actually used them. The climate of the dome didn't fluctuate.

When Juliana got back to the group, her mother, Imogen, was there speaking to Kasperi and father. Workers used clanking pallet jacks to move crates of supplies into the rear of the transport vehicle.

"I don't understand why the children need to go with you," her mother said.

Father was adjusting his exoarmor. Juliana had never seen him wear armor before, and he looked uncomfortable in it. The armor was new and shiny, which contrasted sharply with the numerous cuts and dents on Kasperi's.

"Juliana is nearly ten. At fourteen, she can marry or join the military. It's about time she learns of the outside world," her father said. "I've humored your isolationism long enough. I will not allow the policy to continue with Oliver. My son will learn the way of the world early, like I did."

Mother lowered her voice, and Juliana strained to listen. "When I agreed to come back here, it wasn't to see my children raised on the ice." Then she said something else Juliana couldn't make out. Her mother had an accent like Kasperi's that was sometimes hard for her to understand when she spoke quickly.

Father stepped closer to her mother. Raising his voice, he said, "They are my children, and I will hear no more of it. They will understand what it means to rule. My ancestors conquered these moons, conquered the ice and your barbaric people. They need to understand their legacy like I do. We don't need more Serras who hide in luxurious domes on their estates on Europa and Ganymede."

Juliana tensed. She knew her father's temper well and tried her best to become invisible. He was rarely violent, but his verbal tirades could go on for days, and his foul mood would begin to rub off on everyone else.

He often talked of their family, but none had ever come to visit, and they had never left to see them. Occasionally, Father left to visit Ganymede or somewhere else, but he had always gone alone.

"Lady Serra, I will keep them safe personally," Kasperi said, bowing his head low. Her mother smiled at him, and Juliana thought she never looked that happy with Father.

Her mother kneeled in front of her, draping her scarf loosely around her neck. "Listen to Kasperi, okay?" She pulled Oliver closer to speak to them together. "Both of you. And take care of each other."

"It's okay, Mother. We're only going outside. It's an adventure," Juliana said, trying to show her mother she wasn't afraid.

She smiled back weakly. "Yes, of course it is, dear."

Sometimes Juliana would see other children playing through the dome's distorted energy field. They would dance in the dim light emanating from inside before melting back into the darkness beyond.

They were like figments of her imagination. Cloudy forms that were more of an idea than actual people. Still, she always wanted to join them, hoping to learn their ephemeral secrets.

Except they were never allowed to go outside. Instead, the workers would bring in great big truckloads of snow for them to play with. They would build snowmen and caves to hide in, but they would always melt before bedtime.

She and Oliver would often watch shows on the digiscreen about different places in the solar system. The giant mountains and grassy plains of Mars, the tropical beaches of Venus, and the great deserts of Mercury. None of it was as interesting to her as the jagged ice outside the dome.

Oliver looked afraid, and she squeezed his hand. "It's okay, Oli. Think of all the things we'll see."

He nodded. "Oh yeah, it'll be fun. Maybe..."

"Don't be a baby. Lots of people live out there. Where do you think all the workers live?" she said.

"I like it in here."

"Everyone likes it in the dome. It's warm and safe," Kasperi said. Juliana didn't realize he was still listening. "The ice is beautiful but also very dangerous. It's important to respect the ice."

"Do you miss living outside the dome?" she asked Kasperi.

"No, I've lived many places, but you see my tattoos? My Jeevan." He pointed at the collection of blue lines on his neck and face. "The ink is made from the ice, so it's always with me."

Juliana was surprised he answered. "What do they mean?" she asked, feeling brave. She was always too afraid to ask, but Kasperi was the only person she knew with a Jeevan.

"They're the story of my life. Each Saans, or line, tells a part of my tale. Recorded on my skin for everyone to see and remember. Come on. We should get going."

"Will you tell me what they mean?"

"Maybe one day," he said, shooing them toward the transport.

Juliana had ridden in a transport before to travel from one dome to another but never stopped on the ice. Kasperi helped strap them into their seats before taking his own with the other men. The engines fired on, and they began their departure from the dome.

Juliana

June, 4083 U.E.T. – South Pole, Enceladus

They arrived at their destination in what felt like a long time. The transport landed with a soft thud, and Juliana didn't wait for the lights to turn green before unbuckling her restraints. She was anxious to get moving.

Kasperi quickly motioned her to stay in her seat. Before they left the transport, Father gave her and Oliver another speech about staying with Kasperi, who came to help them put on their masks and fasten their scarves.

"You need to make sure you don't let your skin get too cold. Okay? If you get numb, you need to tell me," Kasperi said.

She looked at Father. "Don't you need a mask too?" He wasn't wearing one or the helmet of his armor.

"The atmosphere is thick enough to breathe. I must meet our workers from a position of strength. Now, no more questions. You three," Father said, flicking his fingers at the workers. "Get these crates unloaded. We're already behind schedule."

Juliana turned back to Kasperi, who was also only wearing light fabric over his head. "Where's your mask?"

"I don't need one. I'm used to the cold," he said kindly. "Come, children, we need to hurry. Remember, stay close. There are crevasses more than a mile deep and strong winds to blow you into them."

Juliana wanted to argue. She didn't need the mask either, but then she looked at Oliver. After that ominous warning, he was even more nervous than before. So she took his hand and followed Kasperi closely. She told herself it was to keep Oliver calm, but she was nervous too, and having him there helped.

Kasperi grabbed the long handle of his lightning pike, releasing it from the transport's wall. Hefting the weapon on his shoulder, he led them outside. She didn't know why he needed a weapon. There weren't any animals outside the dome, as far as she knew, unless the stories they told about monsters were true. But she was pretty sure they weren't.

When the first blast of cold air kissed her cheeks, she forgot about monsters. The air left her lungs from the sharpness, and she had to remind herself to breathe. The wind was powerful, and a burning sensation prickled her exposed skin. The experience was far worse than stepping into a freezer. The sudden jolt caused her and Oliver to stumble.

Kasperi used his large, armored body to block the wind and reached out to steady their steps. "We won't be very long. Forget the cold. Look at the geysers," he said proudly, pointing.

Juliana turned to look, and her mouth hung open beneath her scarf. In the distance were hundreds of plumes of white shooting off into space. Behind them, Saturn and its rings filled almost all her perspective. It shined so brightly that only darkness was visible around it. In that moment, she forgot all about the cold.

"It's like we can touch it," Oliver said, reaching toward Saturn.

Kasperi chuckled. "It's very far away, but it's also very big. It's beautiful, isn't it? A shame you both went this long without seeing it like this."

Juliana had seen photos of Saturn, blurry views through the dome and occasionally clear views from the digiscreen windows. None of it prepared her for the real thing. Her eyes were seeing shades of light and color that cameras couldn't reproduce.

Snow accumulated on her shoulders. She brushed it off while looking for the source since there weren't any clouds. She held out her palm to catch some snowflakes.

"Look closely and you'll see colorful specks," Kasperi said.

"What is it?" Oliver asked, pulling on Juliana's arm to see.

"Minerals from deep in the moon. The snow falls from the geysers and collects here for the workers to mine from the ice," he explained. Oliver seemed more interested than she was.

"It doesn't seem like very much," she said quietly. Closing her fist, she made a small snowball and threw it at Oliver.

Oliver began making his own snowball, but Kasperi stopped him when their father yelled, "Kasperi!"

Kasperi ushered them along quickly.

They moved to a flat area where a collection of small pods was assembled. Kasperi explained they were where the miners lived. Father was already speaking to a group of workers. They were pale-skinned men and women with fair-colored hair like hers, in shades of white to light brown.

They were wearing coveralls that looked much thinner than their own cold-weather gear. Their bodies were likewise thin. Bare faces stared out from under their hoods. Their skin was rough and covered in red patches.

"Are they okay?" she asked Kasperi. He shushed her without turning away from watching Father. Juliana sighed. She hated being ignored by the grownups. She turned to find Oliver but realized he wasn't there.

She spun in every direction looking for him. She would have yelled his name but didn't want to draw any attention to his disappearance.

"Money is coming. For now, you need to keep digging," Father said from behind her. The workers shouted something back in their Armanic language.

She always wanted to learn it so she could speak to the workers inside the dome, but her parents never allowed it. She would speak the Standard tongue and nothing else since it was the language of nobility and the Republic.

Juliana looked to make sure Kasperi wasn't watching before stepping away. She noticed a large digging machine in the distance away from her father. It had a massive articulating arm with a bucket on the end. Ice clung to its body, and it didn't look like it was currently operational. It reminded her of a sleeping bear.

She noticed Oliver standing below the great machine and shuffled toward him. Wary of the crevasses Kasperi warned them of.

"Oli!" she said when she got close. "What are you doing here? We need to stay with Kasperi."

That was when Juliana noticed the other kids standing beside the machine. They had snowballs in their hands and stared at her like she had three heads. The kids pointed at them and said something in Armanic.

"I don't understand," she said, and they all laughed. Juliana put herself defensively in front of Oliver.

"Do you throw?" one of the older kids said in broken Standard. Then he lobbed a snowball at a cluster of icicles dangling from the machine, missing them completely.

"Better than you," she said confidently.

The boy stepped toward her, clenching his fists.

Oliver grabbed her arm, "Come on Juli, let's go. I only wanted to see the machine."

"You throw," the boy said, looming over them.

Juliana turned quickly, thinking she heard shouting behind her. The wind whipped around the machine, and she assumed that must have been what it was. Kasperi might be mad they walked away but they were safe with the other kids, not playing near a crevasse. They wouldn't get punished too badly. Probably.

"It's okay, Oli." To the older boy, she said, "You can throw again."

He grinned, showing off a mouth of chipped yellow teeth. "You first."

Juliana leaned over and made a snowball, but the heavy overcoat made it difficult to bend her arms, so she pulled off her mittens and asked Oli to help her unzip the coat. He hesitated at first and then struggled with the zipper.

"Juli, Kasperi said not to!"

Juliana hushed him, getting the zipper herself and tossing the heavy coat aside on the snow. She was already shivering when she put her gloves back on quickly. It was a cold she wasn't ready for. Back inside the mittens, her hands were stiff and frozen, and she flexed aggressively to get them moving again.

The boy laughed loudly, pointing at her and saying something else in Armanic. She didn't need to understand to know they were making fun of her. She didn't back down because she wanted to show she belonged. Maybe they would even know where Morgan was.

Tightening her jaw, Juliana reached back into the snow. The surface cracked. The snow was turning to ice almost as quickly as it landed. She scooped a layer of fresh snow under the surface and packed it into a tight ball.

She found the largest icicle, aimed, and threw. The snowball launched through the air and hit the icicle perfectly, except it was much too large and thick. Only her snowball shattered on impact.

"Good shot, Juli!" Oliver said cheerfully.

The other kids continued to laugh.

"I show you," the older boy said and threw his own snowball. This time the snowball hit a much smaller single icicle, shattering it into pieces, eliciting a cheer from the other kids.

Juliana huffed loudly. She hadn't known the rules, but she would beat them at whatever game they came up with. She didn't understand why they kept laughing at her. She reached angrily back into the snow. Her body was shaking from the cold, but she didn't care. Winning was more important. She would show them she was at least as good as they were.

Looking up again, she found a small cluster of icicles all side by side. She took aim and threw, hitting the cluster and breaking three distinct icicles. With hands on hips she said, "I win," through chattering teeth.

The boy snarled, his broken teeth giving him a menacing appearance. "You cheated!" he yelled and pushed Juliana. He was much larger than her, and she stumbled backward.

Oliver tried to come to her aid, but she pushed him behind her and dug in. Her body shaking uncontrollably.

"I did not!" she shouted back. Her limbs were going numb, and she thought of what Kasperi had told her, fear rising in her chest.

The boy raised his arm as if to punch her but suddenly stopped. His eyes went wide, and he turned to run, slipping on the ice as he did. The other children stumbled quickly after him.

Then there was a series of loud bangs in the distance. Juliana turned around to see where they came from. She saw her father in the crowd holding something in his hand. There was a man lying still in the snow in front of him.

There was another loud bang, and the miners closed in around their father. They kicked and punched him, throwing him to the ground. She cried out, wanting to help. Some of the miners heard her and came rushing toward them. Juliana looked for Kasperi but didn't see him anywhere.

Juliana grabbed Oliver and ran toward the mining machine. She crawled underneath, pulling Oliver behind her. They needed to hide until Kasperi or Father came back. The machine was large and low to the ground. The space underneath was just large enough for their little bodies to fit under.

She continued to shake from the cold but tried to stay as still as possible. Oliver clung to her sobbing, but the oxygen mask hid the noise.

"Where did the little Imperials go. We can't keep any witnesses," a miner said, their boots crunching on the snow around the machine.

"Let 'em go. They'll die out here anyway. Soft little dome dwellers," the other one said.

Juliana pulled Oliver into her and covered his ears while shutting her eyes tightly. She wished she had more hands to cover her own ears. Her skin prickled with every footfall, and she held her breath, despite the mask.

Suddenly, a strong hand grabbed her, and she screamed, kicking and yelling against the sudden assault while clinging to Oliver.

"Calm yourself!"

The voice was familiar, and Juliana opened her eyes. It was Kasperi by their side. The other men were lying in the snow not far away, a red patch underneath them.

Kasperi pulled her face away. "Come on. We need to get back to the transport."

"What about...father," she asked, barely able to speak from the cold. The crowd was still where he had been, but she didn't see him.

"He will meet us later. Right now, we need to get you both to safety," he said, pulling them up to their feet. "Where is your coat? Never mind, there's no time."

Kasperi nearly dragged them back to the waiting transport. Their short legs, the cold, and the shock made it difficult for them to move any faster. Juliana kept looking back to see if someone was chasing them, but they were alone on the ice.

They found the transport empty. The pilot and other workers they arrived with were missing. Kasperi left them to find their own seats and slammed the cabin door closed before going to the cockpit.

Oliver hurried to his seat like he was instructed but Juliana stood shaking at the door's small window. She watched, stunned, as the ice disappeared beneath them. Her father never reappeared, and she feared what that meant.

She thought of what her teacher had said and realized it was true. This was no place for her. The ice was cold, unforgiving, and not hers to claim.

CHAPTER

4

Events moved too quickly for Juliana to track or ask questions. In a way, the frenetic pace was a blessing because it was impossible for her to dwell on how afraid she was.

Kasperi took them back to the dome, and for a moment she felt safe. The biting wind was gone, and the bright lights warmed her skin. Her world was collapsing, but the familiarity of the dome centered her. It was only a brief respite.

"Go and grab a bag, fill it with whatever you need. You have ten minutes," Kasperi said, dismissing them to their task. He left on his own mission, disappearing into his apartment within the complex.

Obedience had always been expected from her. First from her father, then school, and ultimately the Republic's Universal Church. When a command was given, it was expected to be obeyed. There were times she would argue or bend, but she was too afraid for that now. Juliana jumped into action, grabbing Oliver by the arm and leading him into their home.

They went to their shared bedroom, and she pulled an empty backpack out for each of them. Oliver started to fill his with toys and books while she pulled out clothes and other important things, like her bow and arrow set. If they were in danger, she might need to protect them.

Then she added a pouch full of jewelry. A few bracelets she had made along with gold and silver pieces that belonged to her mother. She took them because she thought they were pretty.

In the common room, she looked at the collection of gems on shelves. They came in a multitude of shapes and colors. A large pink stone in particular caught her eye. It was a gift she had helped mother pick out for father. Juliana tried to grab it before realizing it was too big and heavy. They would have to come back for it.

Juliana didn't understand what was going on, but this part felt routine. They had taken part in regular safety drills that taught them what to do if they had to evacuate the dome. No one ever thought they would need to, but her mother had always stressed that being prepared was important. Now her training was taking over on instinct.

With their bags filled, they moved to their assigned muster point. A few minutes later, Kasperi arrived with Mother. The rest of the property felt strange.

"Where has everyone gone?" she asked. There were always some workers about, but it was like they had all been sent away.

"There's an emergency," her mother said, her face taut. "Children, get into the transport. You don't need to be scared."

Juliana could sense she didn't believe what she said.

Oliver clung to her arm. "Where are we going? Where's Father?" he asked through tears.

"He'll join us soon. We need to go somewhere safe," Mother assured him.

"The dome is safe," Juliana said, looking around.

Everything seemed normal except for the missing people. Her mind went to the image of her father lying in the snow as he was struck by the workers. It occurred to her for the first time that he might be dead.

"Not for very long," Kasperi said, trying to usher them back into the transport. "We need to get somewhere else. Far away from here."

"What's going on?" she asked again. "We need to get Father. Where is he?"

Mother leaned in to put her face close to hers. "There are dangerous people we need to get away from. If we stay here, they'll find us. That's why we need to go quickly. Father will know how to find us. Do you understand? I know you aren't afraid."

Juliana stiffened. "Of course I'm not afraid!"

Kasperi smiled. "Good, then go with your brother and get into the transport. We will follow quickly."

Juliana eventually did as she was told, glad to have another task even if it was watching her brother. Kasperi and Mother hurriedly carried crates of food and equipment onto the small ship. They worked quickly despite the heavy loads they were moving. In the end, the tiny spaceship looked like a stuffed holiday roast.

"Where are we going that we need so much stuff?" Juliana asked when the last bit of equipment was loaded on. "Are we going to Father's family on Ganymede?" Why else would they need so much?

"No," Kasperi said harshly. He slammed the ship's door closed. "We need to go somewhere else."

"We can go to my family," Mother said.

This made Juliana curious because she knew very little about her mother's family. She knew they came from somewhere on Triton but little else. They had never come to visit, and Father had never let them go to Triton.

Kasperi grabbed mother by the arms and said, "That's the first place they will look. We can never go back there. We've already gone over this, Imogen. First, we need to get rid of this ship. They'll be able to easily track it. Then we can consider the next step."

Mother looked even more upset. "I... I wasn't ready."

Kasperi lowered his voice, but Juliana was still able to hear. "You knew this was going to be part of this."

Mother sighed heavily. "So where do we go then?"

Kasperi moved to the pilot's seat. He began turning knobs and pressing buttons. "I know a place on Titan. An old friend there can help us. Everyone, get to your seats."

"Will this transport make it?" Mother asked, worried.

"If we're careful, yes, but it will be an uncomfortable trip."

"How long will that take?" Juliana asked tentatively. She had never taken a trip that lasted more than an hour.

They both looked back in surprise. They hadn't realized she was listening. "It depends on the orbits. I haven't looked at the charts, but at least a week, probably two." Kasperi said, not trying to soften the blow.

"Two weeks!" Oliver shouted. "There's no bathroom here."

Oliver was right. The transport was meant for short excursions. Shuttles between the surface and orbiting spaceships or local trips to neighboring domes.

"What about Father?" Juliana asked again. "Shouldn't we go help him? How will he get back to us?"

Mother and Kasperi exchanged a look. She could guess what they weren't saying. *He's dead.* The realization hadn't sunk in.

"Your father will meet us when he's able. Now get to your seats, go quickly," Mother said. Oliver accepted the answer, but Juliana could tell she was lying.

They didn't linger much longer.

Juliana wanted to see her teacher and friends before they left. If there was danger, didn't they need to leave too? Who was helping them? She didn't understand why they had to leave so quickly.

When they settled into the transport and were safely out in space, she opened the bag of things she had brought. She pushed aside the clothes, taking out the pouch of jewelry. She fingered through the bag, pulling out her favorite pieces.

One of her mother's old bracelets and a necklace she had gotten from her father on the last Illumination Day, a holiday that celebrated the summer solstice on Earth. Why they still celebrated a holiday on a dead planet, she didn't know, but she always liked getting presents.

The necklace was made of gold and shined brightly in the dim artificial light of the craft. She put them on, appreciating the familiar weight. If Father couldn't be there, at least she had the necklace to remember him.

She propped up her bow and arrow beside her. "Mom, do you think I can practice my shooting?"

Her mother turned, shaking her head. "Juliana, did you bring that thing with you? You were only supposed to pack clothes. We've practiced emergency drills how many times? You know this."

"I thought maybe I might need to keep us safe."

Mother sighed heavily, holding her face in her palm. "Maybe when we're out of orbit, if Kasperi says it's okay."

Juliana was glad she agreed so easily. She had received the bow and arrow set a couple of years earlier. When she wasn't studying, she was usually out in the yard shooting at targets beside her father and Kasperi. She had gotten so proficient that she could accurately hit small moving targets from fifty meters or more. It was a skill that had even impressed her father.

After a while, they settled into their journey. They made it out of orbit, and Kasperi set a course for Titan, Saturn's largest moon. They were allowed to unbuckle themselves, and she got to play in zero gravity for the first time until Kasperi activated the gravity generator, which put an end to the fun. It wasn't a very strong generator, so she felt at home, moving with relative ease like she would have in the dome.

Oliver meanwhile seemed content with playing games on his digipad. In his backpack were also a dozen Milton Krane adventure books he brought with him. Juliana was a little annoyed that upon discovering the mountain of books her mother didn't have anything to say about it.

She understood why when her mother opened one of the heavy crates. It was packed to the brim with books from their library. Among them were the especially expensive tomes of ancient history or literature.

They were books with fancy covers that were always locked behind glass cases she couldn't open. They had survived centuries of purges and upheaval when the Republic came to power. Juliana was never allowed to touch them, because no one was supposed to even own them.

Books were her mother's prized possessions, and it was obvious it hurt her that she couldn't take all of them. Without physical books, all they were left with on their digipads were films or other visual media. Unless you wanted to read official Republic histories, the Holy Scripture or technical manuals, physical books were the only option.

From almost the very beginning of their trip, her mother spent most of her time reading or even just looking at her books. Juliana didn't share in her enthusiasm for them, so she spent her time running in place and doing jumping jacks in what little space she had, ignoring the stench emanating from their makeshift toilet.

It didn't stop Juliana from becoming angrier as time passed. Her mother wouldn't acknowledge what happened to Father, and Kasperi remained silent. Oliver became anxious and would cry in fits about wanting to go home, until eventually he grew overwhelmed and fell asleep. Then they all went back pretending nothing had happened.

The journey went on like this forever, each day like the one before. Periods of bickering and tension, interspersed with long stretches of silence. Although, it wasn't all negative. Without her father's tense energy and overbearing nature, they were able to communicate better than they ever had. Eventually, Juliana found comfort in her new routine and tried to forget about what happened.

They arrived at Titan nearly three weeks after they left Enceladus. It turned out the orbits weren't in their favor and Kasperi wasn't a proficient navigator. Mother had never piloted anything and was even less help in getting them to their destination. Things got better once Kasperi worked out the kinks of the automatic charting system.

From the moment they hit Titan's orbit, Juliana was glued to the transport's small window. In the distance was the yellow-tinted sphere of Titan, with Saturn's hulking form and delicate rings lording over it. The planet's swirling clouds looked almost like a painting from a distance. Oliver elbowed her in the ribs to try and get his own glimpse. She eventually relented and let him take over the window.

"Make sure you get a good view," Kasperi said from the pilot's seat. "When we enter the atmosphere, it won't be nearly so pretty."

"Will we be coming back to space?" she asked.

"Hopefully not," Mother answered. She looked a little green and was tapping her feet anxiously. She was well past enjoying the adventure.

Kasperi said, "Soon enough. Take your seats. This might get bumpy."

Juliana's heart fluttered, and she pulled Oliver away from the window. It may have been her mother's fidgeting or the excitement of seeing something new, but she was suddenly very anxious to get to their destination. She could feel the moment they transitioned into the atmosphere. Gravity pulled at her body, pressing her into the seat. She tried to move her hands from her side but didn't have enough strength.

It was loud and bumpy but over within a minute. Thankfully, Kasperi's warnings turned out to be for nothing. He was at least a better pilot than he was a navigator. Their landing was as gentle as any others she remembered, although she barely registered most of the descent. They landed in a small spaceport that Kasperi said was used by local miners and merchants.

She wondered how many places Kasperi had been that he knew so much. She had only ever seen him in the dome, and in that time he had never left. She concluded it must have been part of his time as a soldier, another reason why she would want to do the same one day.

She unbuckled herself from the seat and jumped to test the new gravity. It immediately felt like she was being held down by invisible hands, and she grimaced. She was tangled in an invisible blanket and couldn't find a way out.

Kasperi chuckled from the pilot's seat. "The gravity here is more than Enceladus but much less than Earth standard. You will get used to it." He didn't seem uncomfortable at all.

Juliana hoped he was right. She didn't want to be crushed by the air around her. Mother at least seemed as off balance as she did. She leaned her weight on the cargo to save herself from falling over when approaching her and Oliver, who hadn't unbuckled himself yet. Instead, he was staring off at nothing, a blank expression on his face.

Juliana shook his arm to get his attention, and he came to with a sad smile on his face. She helped him remove the buckles of his restraints.

Mother leaned in close and said quietly, "Before the door opens, remember what we told you. You're Arabella and Jordan Smith now. Do you understand? It's very important."

Juliana studied her mother's face and thought she looked like she might cry. If it made her so sad, why was she doing this? Why did they have to change their names?

"We remember, Mom," Oliver said obediently. She thought he could sense something was wrong. Juliana was certain there was, and she thought she knew the cause.

"If father is coming back, I don't understand why we need new names. And why Smith? Can't we use your name instead? Lowell is a royal name, isn't it? Or why not Kasperi's?" Juliana said, questioning their plan, and not for the first time.

Mother clenched her jaw as if she were trying not to yell.

"Your father—" she began to say.

"Imogen…" Kasperi said, putting a hand on her shoulder.

Mother took a deep breath and said, "We aren't safe here. There are bad people who will come looking for us, the same people who hurt your father. If they catch us, they will take you both away from me." Juliana swallowed the lump forming in her throat. She was angry but she didn't want to lose her or Kasperi. Where would she go? Where would *they*, whoever they are, take her?

Kasperi kneeled in front of them, his scarred and tattooed face as soft as he could make it, which wasn't very soft. "You need to listen to your mother. Your new name will protect you, like I will. No one will take you if you listen."

"What about you? You can't hide your Jeevan. Everyone will know you're Kasperi Nowak."

He smiled softly. "The Jeevan speaks silently. My enemies and friends only need to see it to know my character. It's why people know my face but not my name. Kasperi Nowak is the same as any man. The name doesn't matter, only that we fight for honor and each other. Boisterous words and aggrandized names are for weak men and women who fear their own insignificance."

Juliana didn't really understand what he meant, but she liked that he didn't talk to her like a child. "I understand."

He smiled. "Anyway, your mother and I will both have new names too. Michelle and Alfred Smith."

Juliana frowned. Her mother was her mother and Kasperi would always be Kasperi. She didn't care what he said.

Kasperi rustled Oliver's hair and stood. Turning to their mother, he said, "Once we finish with the local assessor, I'll send word to my cousin. She should be able to arrange a buyer for the transport and provide us with a place to stay for now."

Mother looked them over one last time and raised her hand to her mouth. "Oh no, quick, you need to take those off," she said, fumbling with Juliana's necklace and the bracelets on her wrist. "You need to take these off and hide them. They'll attract attention, and that's not what we need right now."

Juliana was surprised by her aggressiveness, but it left her unwilling to mount a challenge. She stuffed the jewelry into the pocket of her coat. She was sad they had to be put away. It seemed like she was losing everything she had ever known all at once.

A heavy knock came on the transport door. Kasperi entered several commands into the control panel, and the door opened with a hiss as fresh air filled the tiny space for the first time in weeks. Juliana took a deep breath, savoring the freshness.

Standing in front of the opened door was a stoop-shouldered man carrying a digipad. He was flanked by a pair of large and rough-looking men with stun batons at their hips. She assumed this was the assessor Kasperi said would come to meet them.

He wore a simple blue uniform with a plain metal pin on his chest depicting a set of scales and an ID card hanging around his neck. The men flanking him wore patches identifying them as members of the Resident Watch.

The assessor had a general look of disinterest about him that reminded her of being in school. He stepped back abruptly as the likely foul-smelling air from the transport washed over him, his bored expression turning to one of disgust.

"God's bones. Identification," he demanded while fighting to regain his composure.

Kasperi led them out of the transport and into the fresh air of the spaceport. Juliana blinked furiously while her eyes adjusted to the comparatively bright light outside. Nowhere in the Far Coast was bright, of course, outside of domes, but even the darkness of early morning was brighter than the interior of a spacecraft. The effect was made worse by the artificial lights flooding the landing area.

When her vision cleared, she looked around. The spaceport was busy to her eyes. There were half a dozen small transport ships like theirs and at least two much larger ships nearby. Crews of men and women in dirty jumpsuits with reflective stripes hustled from one ship to the next. They connected hoses or moved cargo in and out of the vessels.

One of the workers stopped, leaning against a collection of crates. He pulled out a small flask and tried to drink from it covertly. She watched a large-bellied man approach him, digipad in hand. He wore a clean white helmet and seemed to be in charge. She jumped when he kicked the man in the shin and proceeded to slap the flask from his mouth. The man looked ready to argue, but his coworkers pulled him away, and they got back to work.

Juliana had never seen anything like it, at least not since her father and the ice. She swallowed hard and turned back to Kasperi. She had missed the first part of the conversation.

"We've come from Pandora to register," Kasperi said, naming one of the minor moons of Saturn.

During the journey, Kasperi explained that the minor moons lacked major government services. The communities were often so small, remote, and temporary that it wasn't worth the cost of sending official assessors. Instead, the local magistrates would self-report statistics for their districts. It wasn't uncommon for individuals to be "missed" to avoid population control measures in far-flung colonies.

However military service or education required proper registration, leading to a fairly large number of people occasionally washing up at major ports with no legal documentation.

"In this thing?" the assessor said, looking at the small transport. "You ice rats keep multiplying."

"Driftwood always finds a way," one of the other men said. Then it was as if he noticed Kasperi for the first time and shuffled awkwardly. "No offense meant. You know I served with some of your people once." He coughed when Kasperi didn't answer.

The men looked a lot like them. Light features and pale skin. One of them even had silvery brown hair like Mother's and her own. She supposed their eyes were smaller and their faces less angular, but they weren't *that* different. Anyway, what mattered was they didn't consider themselves Armanic.

The assessor glared at the man and addressed Kasperi. "I can begin your processing, but you'll be grounded until your credentials are cleared through the constable."

"Understood," Kasperi said.

Juliana looked up at the sky during the proceeding. Like Kasperi said, the view was much less beautiful. The yellow tinged atmosphere was too thick to see stars or the hulking form of Saturn. The sun was little more than a distant memory and cast only a soft glow on the moon.

The assessor clicked on a flashlight and looked around the inside of the transport from the door. "Any cargo to declare?"

"None," Kasperi said.

The man narrowed his eyes and stepped into the craft. He used his sleeve to mask the smell. Now that she was able to clear her nose, she could tell their makeshift latrine had become especially ripe. The assessor came out almost right away.

"How long have you been in there?" he asked in obvious disbelief.

"Longer than expected," Kasperi said briskly.

"Sarding hell, don't know how you put up with that, but this is gonna cost you," the assessor said, stepping back outside. "Five hundred credits for the docking fee and another five hundred for the improper storage of human waste."

Kasperi didn't argue and handed the man several credit chips. The assessor looked them over before placing them in his pocket. Satisfied, he moved to look at the registration number on the transport and punched it into his digipad.

His body tensed, and he looked up. "Did you say you were coming from Pandora?"

Oliver became uneasy and clung to Juliana, who in turn moved closer to their mother. She wrapped an arm around them but didn't say anything.

"Yes, is there a problem?" Kasperi said softly.

The armed guardsmen reached for their weapons, and the assessor waved them back. He looked around the spaceport before stepping closer to Kasperi.

"For ten thousand credits, there doesn't need to be."

"Five"

"Eight," the assessor countered. "You can't fight us all and get back out of here."

There was a long pause.

Kasperi reached into his pocket slowly and pulled out more credit chips.

"Usually, ice rats aren't so smart. Come into the office and we can take care of your registration papers. Just keep those little brats in line. This isn't the ice. It's civilized here."

Was he talking about us? Her face was flushing. She wanted to scream and tell the man what he said wasn't true. He needed to know they weren't ice rats. They weren't bad people.

Her mother clenched her arm in warning, and Juliana kept her mouth shut. She didn't understand why Mother wouldn't say something. She was a noble and should be treated like one. Everyone knew that.

Instead, they walked meekly into the office behind the official. No one paid them any attention, except for passing glances. She wasn't used to being so invisible.

CHAPTER
5

Juliana

July, 4083 U.E.T. – Notus City, Titan

It was in that crowded and dirty clerk's office where Juliana died.

The office was busier than any place in the dome. People sat shoulder to shoulder on long benches, waiting for their turn to be seen by the local constable. There were crying babies, coughing elders, and the overpowering smell of unwashed bodies permeating the air. She sniffed her clothes and realized the smell might have been them.

A bright light flickered on and off overhead. It struggled to remain lit, like the desperate people around them struggled to remain optimistic. Some had hopeful smiles, but most looked on the verge of tears.

The collective energy of the room was coiled tightly, threatening to burst out at the slightest touch. It seemed like all of them were being forced into a new life they wanted no part of. Watching over them were portraits of the Vox and Manus on the wall.

The exterior windows were so dirty they only let in diffused light from the lamps outside, which added to the gloomy atmosphere. Along the opposite wall was a single glass window behind metal bars. A clerk sat distributing stacks of papers through an opening that was barely big enough. Maybe they thought if it was any bigger it might allow in whatever disease they all carried.

The assessor went to the window, pushing aside a man who was mid conversation. He retrieved a stack of papers and brought them back to Kasperi.

"Fill these out and wait here. You'll be called when it's your turn," he said and then disappeared into the rear office.

Kasperi pulled them into the only empty space left in the cramped room. He and Mother looked over the paperwork while Juliana looked around the room, keeping an eye on Oliver clinging to her side.

She watched people visit the clerk's window, before returning to their seats. Many stared at the paperwork with confused expressions. Their hopelessness was familiar to her. It was how she felt when her teacher handed her some impossible exam. She considered they might not be able to read.

Even those who managed to fill out the paperwork would have to make the line all over again. If there were any issues, they would be sent back to their seats to correct them before starting the process all over again.

Those who got it right were still left waiting until someone came out from behind the wall to call them into the backrooms. In the time it took Mother and Kasperi to fill out the paperwork, she hadn't seen anyone who entered leave the building.

When they were done, Kasperi said, "It will be okay here for now." He handed the stack of papers to Mother. "I need to go and find my cousin Lena. She'll be able to help us. I won't be long."

Oliver jumped onto his leg. "I don't want you to go!"

Mother pulled him back. "Shh. We can't yell, Jordan. It's going to be okay. Alfred will be right back."

"Father never came back!" he said, drawing the attention of others in the room. Mother was mortified.

"Jordan!" Juliana said, trying to get his attention. "What if we go outside? We can look at the other starships. You like those."

He looked back to Kasperi and then her. He was breathing fast, and Juliana could relate to how he felt. They were all struggling to keep it together. Juliana looked to Mother and Kasperi for permission. She wanted to be anywhere but inside the cramped government office.

Mother shook her head aggressively. "No, it isn't safe outside."

Kasperi put up his hand to stave off a new round of arguments. "I have an idea." He approached the man nearest them on the bench. With a soft whisper and the exchange of a credit chip, he gave up his seat.

Kasperi wiped at the dirty window with his sleeve and then easily lifted

Oliver onto the bench. From there, he could see the ships outside the window. "Here, there's room for both of you. I'll be back soon."

It wasn't the same as going outside, but Oliver looked excited. She could pretend to be happy for him, like she had pretended to be brave.

Mother held out a hand, as if she was going to stop Kasperi but pulled away. Turning her back on him, she came to hover over them protectively.

"There are so many people," Oliver said, his face plastered to the window.

"So many more than in the dome," Juliana added.

"Titan is a big place. It's the largest moon of Saturn and the capital of the Saturnalian province. It's where the archbishop lives, along with the duke and duchess," Mother explained.

"Will we get to meet them?" Juliana asked.

Mother smiled sadly. "No, dear."

Juliana whispered, "But Father's a lord. Can't we see the duke and duchess at least? We don't need to try and see the archbishop if that's not okay."

"No," Mother snapped. "You can't say things like that. We're Smiths, not lords, clergy, or anyone else important."

After that, Juliana didn't bother to ask any more questions. Oliver was content to spend the time watching the ships in the spaceport. Most were small transports or cargo carriers. They landed quickly, unloading passengers or crates before returning to the sky in a delicate dance of organization.

They were called to the counter after a time. Kasperi hadn't returned, but Mother took their hands and led them up to the barred window. The clerk behind the glass looked at them with distracted impatience. It was the way her father looked at workers around the dome. There was no greeting or warmth. This was the first time Juliana had ever had someone look at her that way.

The official said several things to Mother she couldn't hear before looking down to Juliana. "Name."

"Arabella, Arabella Smith," Juliana said weakly. First she lost her home, and now she lost her name.

The woman looked her up and down and then looked at Oliver. "And that must be Jordan Smith?"

Mother nodded, and the woman entered the details on her digipad. She exchanged a few more words with mother, credit chips were handed over, and they were led into the back without having to wait any longer in the crowded room.

In the back, another clerk took them to a small booth where they posed for photos. When it was her turn, Juliana smiled the way she would for holiday photos.

"What're you doing? Close your mouth," the man said with annoyance.

Juliana snapped her lips closed. She was embarrassed and confused, but the man didn't care.

When the photos were taken, he waved them to another small waiting area. There they sat for thirty minutes until eventually a female clerk arrived with identification cards she handed to Mother.

"Welcome to civilized society. You should try and teach your bastards the Standard tongue. Will help them not end up like you."

Mother nodded silently.

"We already speak Standard," Juliana said angrily. "And we aren't bastards."

The woman snorted. "Sure, you aren't. Bet your daddy's off on some asteroid fighting the Vermilion Coalition, right?" she said, looking back at Mother. "Better not to lie to 'em either, you know. Nothing wrong with how you make your money. I might have done the same if I was as pretty as you."

Mother's face grew red, and she looked ready to cry. Luckily, it was then Kasperi returned. The clerk took a step back, appraising him with a harumph. "Guess I was wrong. Armanic war brood after all. Could have sworn you were a common whore."

Kasperi clenched his jaw and put a hand over Juliana's mouth. The clerk laughed, and Kasperi took them quietly back outside. Apparently, he already had his new identification. Juliana was glad they could leave.

Mother was crying now, and Juliana tried to hold her hand. "Why was she so mean? You aren't any of those things. You're a princess."

Mother sniffled, trying to compose herself. "Yes, dear. Thank you."

Kasperi lead them back to their transport where a new man and woman stood talking. The man wore a large scarf over his head and neck, and his skin was tan like her teacher's had been. He was quite large with a bulging belly that strained the fabric of his shirt.

Kasperi spoke quietly. "The woman is my cousin, and the man is an agent for a Mercurian businessman. He's going to buy the transport. Say nothing."

Mother held them back a few paces away so Kasperi could manage their business. They were, however, close enough that Juliana could still hear. She held Oliver's hand as he stayed more interested in looking at the ships landing and taking off around them.

"Lena tells me you want to sell your transport," the Mercurian said in a strange accent.

Kasperi said, "I'd rather trade it for a cargo ship."

The man looked the ship over. "It's a nice vessel. It could be used for shipping light cargo. Why do you want to trade it?"

"We would prefer something larger and more suited to heavy freight than passengers."

The man crossed his arms. "Do you have documents for it?"

"No. Is that a problem?" Kasperi replied, crossing his much-larger arms.

The Mercurian looked like he might laugh. "No, but it'll hurt the price of course. Let me talk to my boss." He walked a distance away to talk to another man.

He looked older but vibrant, wore brightly colored robes, and his hair was pulled tightly back on his head. He carried a golden cane that he leaned on lazily. The artificial light of the spaceport sparkled on the jewels of his rings.

The scarfed man spoke into his ear, and the old merchant simply waved in reply. The scarfed man returned a moment later with an offer. "He says you can have that ship over there."

They all looked in unison to where he pointed. It was a larger ship covered in rusty panels and singe marks. The hull was peppered with dents and gouges. It looked like it had been used as target practice for a long time.

"Will that even fly?" Juliana said, perhaps echoing everyone's thoughts. They turned back to the Mercurian for a reply.

"She isn't pretty, but she's a good workhorse."

"I think you can do better," Kasperi said with a sigh.

His cousin Lena was quick to jump in. "Hey, it's a good deal. Let's not overthink this, alright?"

The scarfed man grinned with a chuckle. His fat giggled. "Listen to yer cousin, big guy. I don't think you want to go through official channels, do you? But if you want, we can reach out for the official documents."

Kasperi exhaled and held out his arm reluctantly. The man took it, and they completed the deal.

When the pair of Mercurians were gone, they walked toward their new ship. Up close, it somehow looked even worse.

"It's not bad for a piece of shit," Lena said, and mother scowled at her. "Ah right, Kasp told me you think you're some princess. Well, I hate to be the one to tell you, but the Armanic Republic's been dead and gone for centuries. You aren't any better than the rest of us. Yer all still ice rats."

"Thats not true!" Juliana shouted. Why did everyone keep saying such horrible things?

"Ha, teaching them fantasies too. They're in for a rude awakening. The world's a shitty place, kid. Time to get used to it, if you're ever going to make anything of yourself. Not much choice with this situation of yours."

Juliana didn't understand what she was saying but also didn't know why her mother wasn't speaking. Why wasn't she yelling at this horrid woman and telling her she was wrong and none of the things she said were true?

Kasperi stepped between them. "That's enough, Lena. Thank you for arranging that meeting, but we can take it from here." He handed her several credit chips.

Lena smirked and handed him a piece of paper. "Pleasure doing business, cousin. You can use this address. It's not far from here. Rent's due on the first. You can pay Mr. Chen in the shop underneath. Don't be late with the payments. I don't need you making me look bad. I don't care if you're family—I'll sell you out if you do." With that she left them.

Oliver looked frightened, and Juliana tried to calm him down. Meanwhile, Mother helped Kasperi move their few crates of belongings from the old transport to their new rust bucket.

Juliana was glad it was much larger, but it also smelled of mold and tobacco smoke. The seats were all bare metal, the cushions having been torn out a long time prior. It would need a lot of repairs to be even a fraction as comfortable as the transport was. She struggled to find any positives until finally saying, "At least there's a toilet."

It was the right thing to say at that moment, and they all shared a laugh. The tension noticeably decreased. Their situation was new and chaotic, but Juliana was trying to see the adventure in it. Even if everyone they met was rude and nasty. Kasperi was being brave, so she would be too.

They left their new ship locked up with most of their belongings in the spaceport berth. From there, they went on foot to visit their new home. Kasperi carried a large box. They would come back for the rest of their belongings.

The city streets were crowded, reminding Juliana of shows on the digiscreen about life in the busy cities of Mars or other planets in the Inner System. She wasn't sure how the population of Titan compared, but at that moment she couldn't imagine a busier place.

Bright lights from a multitude of street signs lit the otherwise dim streets. Unlike the dome, there was no artificial sunlight overhead. Instead, there was perpetual twilight over everything, even in the afternoon. It was like God draped a blanket over the Sun. The thick yellowish haze of the atmosphere only made the situation worse. Blocking even a view of Saturn.

They were pushed and jostled as they walked, and mother was forced to pick up Oliver while Kasperi pushed open a path for them. In the press, Juliana lost her grip on her mother's hand and was almost left behind when she stopped to look at a merchant preparing some kind of food.

What he was making was brightly colored like candy and dripped what looked like honey. It smelled like the holidays, and her mouth watered, especially after so much time in space eating dry ration bars. She asked if they could try one, but her mother quickly pulled her away.

For the rest of the journey, she was forced to walk between Mother and Kasperi. They would push her along if she tried to stop and stare at any of the new sights. Juliana got the feeling her mother felt uncomfortable interacting with the local people.

When locals got close, Mother would shy away, avoiding eye contact and not responding. Kasperi looked far more at ease, and Juliana tried to model her own behavior after his.

After what felt like an eternity but was likely only a few minutes, they came to a quieter street. It was little more than an alleyway with barely enough space for two adults to walk shoulder to shoulder. At the end of that alley was a small store.

The store was nearly overflowing with all manners of packaged food stuff, beverages, tobacco, trinkets, and home goods. Juliana recognized it was a store but had never seen one like it in real life. The dome didn't have any need of stores.

Basic goods were delivered in regular shipments. But there was still the occasional market day where merchants would come to set up tables with goods for sale. Mostly handmade crafts or other luxuries. Juliana always loved market days.

Outside the store, an old man sat on a bucket. His skin was a paler white than her own, and his head was bald and spotted from age or radiation. He was placing white and black stones on a game board by himself. He paused to wave at them when they got closer.

"New tenants?" he said, looking up from the game.

Kasperi acknowledged that they were.

"Stairs are there," he said, motioning to an even narrower doorway beside his store front. "Name's Chen. Been here all my life. If you need anything while you get settled, come see me. I can offer some credit if you need it."

He had a heavy accent and, coupled with the high pitch of his voice, was difficult to understand.

"Thank you, but we won't be here very long," Mother said, and the man nodded deeply.

"I understand. Most people say something like that, but if you change yer mind, you know where I am. Place ain't half bad."

"Do you own it?" Kasperi said.

"Nah, but the same guy owns my stall. I've been renting from him for more than thirty years. He's an old magnate, not a bad guy. I look after the place for him since he doesn't come here often. Keeps the rent fair, despite the rationing. Keeps people sticking around."

"What happened to the last tenant?" Mother asked.

"Dead in the Midnight Raids," Chen said matter-of-factly. Juliana didn't know what he meant, but Mother and Kasperi seemed sad. "Glad that business is over, at least for now."

The grownups agreed, and her family continued up the narrow staircase. They found the door to their new home at the top. It was sheltered under a flimsy piece of bent metal. The door was heavily scratched, dented, and covered in rust. It looked like it hadn't been opened in years.

Kasperi scanned the access card, and the door groaned. It opened slowly, particles of rust flaking off. Juliana worried once they went inside the door might never open again. Kasperi stepped in first, and the rest of them followed tentatively.

Their new home was almost no bigger than the transport ship they had used to get to Titan. It was dim and dreary and turning on the lights only made it worse. There was more rust than paint on the bare metal walls. The plastic trim showed obvious signs of wear. A thick layer of dust clung to everything, including the moth-eaten furniture. Spiders and who knew what else likely made their homes in the darker recesses. It was dirtier than a storage shed back in the dome.

Oliver cried almost immediately, clinging to Mother's leg. Juliana wanted to do the same but swallowed hard. She still needed to be brave. "I can help clean," she announced.

Mother took a deep breath, and the tears at the corners of her own eyes resisted the pull of gravity. "Go ask Mr. Chen for some supplies," she said, handing Juliana a credit chip.

Kasperi set down the box he was carrying. "I'll go and collect the rest of our things," he said, giving Mother's arm a squeeze.

Juliana grabbed Oliver by the hand. "Come on, Ol... Jordan. I'm going to need your help to carry everything." She wanted to be helpful and show she was strong and brave, even if she didn't feel it.

She modeled her behavior by mirroring Kasperi but heard her father's voice in her mind. She remembered something he would say every time she complained or cried. He didn't know how to comfort, so instead he instructed. It was one of the last things that connected her to him.

He would say, "Remember that you cannot wallow in despair. You can't sit wishing for the world you deserve and lament no one has given it to you. It is up to you to fight for it, to grasp it from the maw of the universe. The future is yours for the taking, if you're strong enough to hold it."

Not for the first time, she thought about what happened to him back on the ice. He had never been warm or tender, but she felt deep sadness at his absence. He was her father, and that was enough for her to care. She assumed he was dead, even if the concept was abstract to her. She never knew anyone who died. People went away and never came back. She guessed death was something like that.

Then she thought of her new name, Arabella. She always liked the name Juliana. It was her grandmother's name, but they never met. Now, the loss of the name felt like dying too. Juliana was being left behind to keep her father company. She hoped he would like that. Maybe in this world Arabella still had a father who loved her, and that thought brought her some comfort. Even if it was a lie.

CHAPTER

6

Arabella, with Jordan in tow, followed Kasperi outside to the old man's shop. She still couldn't think of him as anything but Kasperi. They waited quietly while he said something softly to Mr. Chen, who nodded. The old man turned to Arabella and held out a hand.

"What do you have for me, kid?"

It took her a moment to realize what he meant before handing over the credit chip. Life inside the dome was much simpler. They always had what they needed. Even on market days, Mother would handle everything, and she never thought about money.

The man took the credit chip while humming to himself. He began pulling out various items, like sponges, cleaning cloths, and small brushes. He piled them up on the tiny counter.

"Start taking all of this upstairs and come back for more."

They did as they were told, taking as many of the items as they could in their small hands. They came back for the large broom, mop, and bucket. Finally, there were only two large jugs left for them to take. Streaks of blue liquid stained the sides of the bottles, and they smelled oddly sweet. She assumed it was some kind of cleaning solution.

Wanting to get the task over with she carelessly pulled one of the jugs off the counter from its handle. She was excited to help at first, but now she wanted to be done so she could go to bed. Maybe then she could wake up somewhere else far away from this awful place.

The jugs were much heavier than she expected. The first one made her

49

body sway off balance, but she reached for the second one anyway. She got it off the edge of the counter, but the handle was greasy. It slipped from her hand and crashed loudly into the old man's Go board. White and black stones flew in every direction, clattering into the alley.

The jug of cleaning solution rolled to a stop. The cap was missing, and blue liquid coated everything. The old man began to yell, but Arabella was too stunned to move. He barreled past her to try and contain the spill while continuing to curse loudly.

It was the last straw she could handle. All of it was a step too far. She became dizzy, and a heavy sense of dread washed over her. She vaguely remembered Jordan tugging on her arm, but it didn't help.

She had to get away from this horrible place. It was all her mother's fault. She had brought them here against their will to escape some invisible monsters that never came. They should never have come here. Why couldn't they stay in the dome where it was bright and warm, where color existed and they were happy?

Arabella didn't know what else to do, so she shoved past the old man and ran into the alley. She didn't know where she was going but knew she had to leave. The air was thick on Titan and burned her lungs. The yellow haze and dim light added to the dream-like quality. There was no clear sky, simulated or otherwise, to guide her. It was a drab nightmare that refused to end.

She ran out into the main street and bumped into distracted pedestrians. They checked their pockets before pushing her away and cursing her as a thieving urchin. One man even pulled back his arm as if to strike her, but she was quick enough to dodge and run away to the nearest alley she could find.

She continued to run, her breath heavy. She was small, and so it was easy to duck below the wires and pipes. The alleys served as utility corridors and reminded her of similar ones she had explored in the dome. It was a welcome comfort amidst her uncertainty. These were the forgotten places she could hide with her dreams and memories. In that moment she hoped no one would ever find her again.

Except the longer she moved, the less it seemed to help and the more anxious she became. She had run away, but for what? Where would she go? She didn't even know where she was. She began to cry and searched frantically for a way out of the maze of narrow corridors. The peace of the past moment replaced with terror from a new perspective.

On instinct, she moved and clawed toward an escape. Finally emerging into a slightly larger corridor containing a multitude of doors. Tears streamed down her face, and she picked one of the two directions available to her at random. She only made it a half-dozen steps before one of the doors opened and a man stepped out carrying a mop bucket.

She crashed into him, and he yelled. The bucket fell from his hands and clattered on the pavement.

Arabella landed hard on her knee, and she could feel the scrape without looking at it. She screamed, but it wasn't from the pain of the injury. She crawled away from the stranger and curled herself into a corner like a frightened mouse. She wrapped her hands around her legs and buried her face into them, wishing she could disappear.

"Hey, relax, it's okay," the man said, holding his arms out.

Arabella sobbed, keeping her face buried. She was too tired to run anymore but also too scared to face whoever this new person was. She couldn't be brave anymore.

She felt an arm on her shoulder and flinched. The man quickly removed his hand. "Hey, are you okay? Looks like you hit your knee pretty good there."

"I... I'm sorry about your bucket," she whimpered.

"Oh, it was mop water. I was going to dump it out anyway. I'm sorry about your knee."

She looked up when he didn't continue to yell. He had a youthful face like Mother but looked younger than Kasperi. He was also the first person who had spoken kindly to her since she got here. "I don't know where I am."

"Okay..." he said, seemingly thinking. "Well, have you had anything to eat? We can figure out where to bring you back to. I wish Maggie were here. She would know what to do."

Arabella's stomach growled, and she shook her head. It had been a while since they last had a meal. "No, I haven't."

"Come on in. You can be one of my first customers. I just bought this place. It's not much from back here in the alley, but this is my tavern." He sounded quite proud.

Arabella was about to say yes, and then she remembered she had no credit chips. "I don't have any money."

"It's okay. This one's on me," he said warmly.

She was thankful for his kindness and didn't argue. He led her inside, and she was greeted by a new world of bright color. The walls of the hallway were clad in vibrant wallpaper with floral designs in various shades of red and green.

"It's pretty, isn't it? My wife Maggie picked it out. She knows all the names of these flowers here," he said, pointing to some of the different ones in the pattern. "I'd have her tell you about them, but she's out working right now."

They stepped into another room near the back door. Inside was a small apartment. It was a similar size to her family's new home but infinitely cleaner. There was a comfortable sitting area, a small table, and a door leading into the back. It was clean and tidy but otherwise unadorned.

"Take a seat at the table. I'll fetch you something from the kitchen," he said, walking through the door and into a short hallway.

She sat and reflected on how much more normal things felt inside the little apartment. It was easy to forget she wasn't in the dome, and that helped her relax. By the time he returned with a bowl of soup, her tears were gone.

He set the bowl down, and she dug into it ravenously.

The man laughed, "It's okay. I won't take it away from you. You can take your time."

The soup was mostly broth with only a couple of small chunks of vegetables inside, but it was the first warm meal she had in weeks. Everything about it was delicious.

The man sat down across from her. He waited silently until she slowed down in her eating and asked, "What's your name, kid?"

"Ju...Arabella" she said, catching herself.

"Jurbella?" he repeated with a raised eyebrow.

"No… Just Arabella," she said, and he nodded in understanding.

"That's a pretty name. I had a cousin named Arabella actually. My name's Finn."

"It's nice to meet you," she said politely. With the food in her stomach, she began feeling more like her normal self. She also began to realize she shouldn't be here. Mother was never going to let her leave that dirty old apartment again.

"Aren't you polite," he said, leaning back in his chair. "You said you didn't know where you were before. Where are you from?"

The question made her more uneasy. The warnings Kasperi and Mother had given her echoed in her mind. She had to be careful what she said and to whom she said it. "Pandora. We just got here."

"Oh, that's a long way. Welcome to Titan. What brings you guys here?"

"My dad is a transporter. He said there's more work here on Titan for shipping," she said, repeating what Kasperi had taught her to say. She wanted to be polite but knew she had to leave. Only, she still didn't know how to get back.

His face lit up and he said, "Oh, there sure is. My wife Maggie actually manages a logistics company. It's why she's away right now. Maybe I can connect her with your father. She's always looking for more pilots."

Arabella smiled. It sounded like he would know where the spaceport was. Bringing back the information about Maggie might even help her avoid being locked away in their apartment. Mother and Kasperi were going to be very angry she ran off. "I think he would like that. Are you Armanic?"

He nodded. "I am," he said and added something else in Armanic.

She looked down at her hands, embarrassed. "I don't know what you said."

"Ah, I thought you asked because you are too. It's okay," he said, maybe trying to cheer her up. She didn't bother correcting him. "Did you, uh, get separated from your parents or something? I can call the Resident Watch, and they could help you find them."

She stood abruptly at the mention of the Watch, startling Finn. Kasperi said they should trust the Watch least of all.

"No, I got distracted and went the wrong way. I need to get back to the spaceport. It shouldn't be far, right?"

"Oh... No, it's not that far at all. You sure you're okay going alone? I can lock up and show you if you want."

"No!" she shouted nervously. What if he still contacted the Watch? "That's okay. If you tell me the way, I can find it."

He seemed to think about that a long time before agreeing. "Alright, when you get back to your dad, let him know to come see me, okay?"

She agreed to do that, and he went about explaining the way to go. Finn even packed a large container of soup in a bag for her to take back for everyone else. She wished everyone on Titan could be as friendly as Finn. He reminded her of her teacher.

Arabella felt better now that she had a full belly. She also found new confidence after convincing Finn not to call the Watch. It was still difficult to navigate the crowds and noise, but the directions were easy to follow.

She bumped into several people as she gawked at the hoverbikes or hid in corners to avoid the patrolling Watchmen. They didn't seem to pay her any attention, but she was still nervous.

The people she bumped would immediately check their pockets, but no one tried to hit her again. She decided to make it a game to see how far she could go without attracting anyone's attention, a fun distraction from how scared she was.

There were so many people. It was amazing to think they could all be in one place at one time. They went in and out of residential buildings or stopped at one of the many street merchants for food or other wares. Each one of them, going about their lives without care for the crowds around them. The more she explored, the more she opened herself up to the new experience.

It was overwhelming but also wonderful. She knew from the digiscreen there were huge cities on planets like Mars and Venus. The dome was so different that she never imagined there would be anything like it here on the moons of Saturn. She even saw a vendor with real Pandora Fleet jackets on display.

On her favorite shows, the heroes were always Pandora Fleet members. Growing up on Enceladus, even in the dome, everyone wanted one of those jackets. There was a fleet base located there, but it was on the other side of the moon, and Arabella had never visited. However, one day she would have a jacket of her own. It was something not even Kasperi had.

From her new perspective, the neon lights of the storefronts cast a beautiful rainbow over everything. The colors were so bright and vibrant that they cut through the perpetual gloom, leading her back to where she was supposed to be, albeit slowly. On her own, she could admire the mysteries of this place without Kasperi or Mother pushing her along.

Juliana wondered how Milton Krane felt when he first set foot on these barren moons long ago before people called the Far Coast home, even before space stations hung in orbit over the surface. She imagined it must have been scary to be so alone and so far from home. He did it though and paved the way for everyone there. When she got scared, she would have to remember that.

Close to the spaceport, she crossed paths with Kasperi. He was leaving the secure area with another crate in his arms. He stopped in surprise at seeing her. "What are you doing out here? You're supposed to stay with your mother." His tone was harsh, like she knew it would be.

"I... There was an old man, and then..." She was trying to think up some lie to tell him, but nothing came quickly enough. "I was scared and ran. I'm sorry." She hung her head and averted her eyes.

His tone softened slightly. "Let's get back. I'm sure your mother is worried."

Arabella felt a little bit bad about that, but only a little. It was still her mother's fault that they were here at all. Kasperi walked several steps ahead, but she didn't follow. Others moved around her with huffs and quiet expletives. Thankfully they only called her an ice rat once before noticing Kasperi's imposing figure.

Kasperi stopped and set the crate down away from the stream of humanity. He came back to pull her by the arm out of the road. No one paid them more than a quick glance. It was still a normal day for everyone else.

"Come here and sit. I know it's been a difficult day."

Arabella dragged her feet but took a seat on the crate and buried her face in her palms. She wanted to cry, but no tears came. Even the lights of the city weren't interesting anymore. The momentary wonder vanished when reality returned. "I don't want to be here. Why did we have to leave? Why couldn't we stay and wait for father? Where is he?"

Her questions came out like water from a broken faucet.

Kasperi took a knee beside her so he could be at her level. "I know it's scary, but it will get better with time. Those men back on the ice were your father's enemies. They would come looking for you and your brother. That's why we needed to leave."

She barely listened to his excuse. "No one even wants us here. Why do they keep insulting us? Even you with your Jeevan."

Kasperi's face grew stiff, his eyes heavy. "To be Armanic is to be reviled." His voice became a whisper. "There was a time we ruled planets and moons like the Republic, but that was long ago. Those who don't share our history have been told lies about us. They're jealous they don't share our noble blood."

He was speaking of the secret histories of their people shared in whispers and stolen glances. The tales written in ink passed down from generation to generation. It was a history buried in the ice. The only part of Armanic culture appreciated by the Republic now was their aptitude for war.

She raised her head from her hands to look at him. "None of that matters anymore. No one cares," she said angrily. "I don't even speak Armanic. It isn't my history. My father isn't Armanic either. He's a Solite!"

In the digiscreen shows, people from the Far Coast were all lumped together. Anyone with pale skin from the Jovian moons to Pluto were all labeled Armanic, but that wasn't the reality. The Armanic people were only one ethnic group among many.

The ice people were numerous once, but they were no longer the majority in the Far Coast. There were millions of Solites among the population that claimed ancient origins somewhere in the Inner System.

She hadn't really understood the distinction before, because almost everyone who was in the dome was Armanic. Those who weren't worked for her father and had always treated them the same. In one day on Titan, she realized how dumb she had been. Being Armanic also meant being less than, at least until she was old enough to hold a rifle.

Kasperi looked sadder than she'd ever seen him. "No, you're wrong. The same blood that defeated emperors and conquered moons flows through your veins. Ancient blood from your mother. That makes you Armanic, even if your father wasn't. To be Armanic is more than ice and war. It's honor, faith, and upholding justice."

She wasn't sure she agreed with him. What did blood matter when words were what people could hear? Her pale skin and large eyes were what people would see.

There wasn't anything else she wanted to say. Kasperi wasn't making her feel any better. Like her father told her, she would have to find her own way.

When they got back to the old man's store, Kasperi pushed her forward, and she crossed her hands, head bowed slightly. "I'm sorry," she said weakly, anticipating Mr. Chen's imminent anger.

The blue liquid on the street was already mopped away, and Mr. Chen was polishing his Go pieces one by one with a small rag.

Calmly he said, "Help me clean the pieces and it'll be okay."

Arabella could see her mother standing at the top of the stairs leading to their apartment. The look of relief on her face was plainly visible. Arabella avoided making eye contact with her.

"Yes, sir," she said, moving to do as he asked. Kasperi seemed pleased and continued up the stairs with the crate of their belongings.

"Have you ever played Go before?" Mr. Chen asked.

Arabella was still confused about why he wasn't yelling at her. "No...but aren't you mad?"

The old man shrugged. Up close he seemed more youthful than she would have expected. "You're a child, not a dog. I would rather teach you to be more careful than hit you with a stick." He placed a white stone in the appropriate bowl with a sigh. "I was never any good at training dogs or children, but I still try. That's the whole point of Go. The cultivation of strategy, patience and adaptability toward the ultimate goal."

Something about his delivery and his willingness to treat her like more than a child sucked Arabella in. "What's the ultimate goal?" she asked. Her anticipation for what deep wisdom he would give her next was palpable.

He spoke a few words in Armanic she didn't understand.

When she didn't answer, his lips parted, revealing a toothy, yellow smile. "To beat your enemy, of course. It's an old saying. You don't speak your own language?" He clicked his tongue in disapproval. "Such a problem with today's youth."

"I'm not Armanic. I'm Saturnalian. From En... Pandora," she quickly corrected herself.

The old man looked her over, squinting. "Your father has a Jevan, and your mother looks like she just stepped off the ice with her long features and that silver hair. Maybe there's something of the Empire in your nose, but you're still Armanic alright. I'm never wrong about this."

Heat rose in her cheeks, and she balled her fists. She wasn't sure why she was getting mad. Before they left Enceladus, she wanted to be like Kasperi, but then the clerk at the spaceport looked at her like she was contagious.

Now this old man said she wasn't Armanic enough because she didn't speak their stupid language. Didn't Kasperi say her blood was all that mattered? There were too many rules, and she was beginning to hate everyone for it. Why did they care so much to put a label on her?

"I'm Saturnalian. That isn't my father. My father was Jovian," she said, her voice cracking.

Chen nodded as if it all made sense now. "Maybe you were born on a Saturnalian moon, like your father was born on a Jovian one, but you can still be Armanic. Culture is about more than where you're born. It unites us, even if we're far apart, unlike the Republic's planetary tribalism."

Now she had no idea what he was talking about. He must have realized the same thing. "Come on, sit and play. I'll teach you the game and the language of your people, even if you want to deny it."

She hesitated, deciding whether to run up the stairs into the apartment instead.

"It's part of your punishment for nearly destroying my shop earlier," Mr. Chen said with a raised eyebrow.

Arabella grudgingly pulled up another bucket and sat across from him. "Were you born on the ice?"

"I was born right here on Titan. Not much ice compared to Enceladus or Triton, but being Armanic is about more than the ice, you know," he said, pointing a boney and misaligned finger. "There are Armanics everywhere from Mercury to Pluto. Have been since before the Empire."

All she knew about the Solar Empire was that it existed a long time ago. The Republic defeated them and set the nine worlds on a godly path. Never in her lessons had she heard anything about the Armanic people existing in those times. That they came from places other than the ice moons was even more far-fetched.

He may have been lying, but she didn't care. She hung on his every word and listened closely as he began his lesson on how to play Go. The lesson was made harder by the fact he was giving half of his instructions in Armanic.

The next five years were a murky pool in her memory. The one thing that stood out to her during that time was the true nature of their situation. Juliana embraced her new identity as Arabella and became increasingly aware that the events leading up to their escape from Enceladus weren't completely random.

She spent years reconstructing the events. What had seemed like an opportunistic attack on her father by angry miners began to coalesce into a complex plot by her mother to eliminate an abusive and foreign husband, replacing him with an honorable and sympathetic lover from her own Armanic community.

Arabella had no way to prove any of this was true, but the love Kasperi showed for her mother Imogen seemed deep and prolonged, at least once she was old enough to notice the signs. Stolen smiles, manufactured attempts at privacy, and intimate embraces when they thought she and Jordan were asleep.

It all felt too passionate to have grown randomly like a weed. Their love was plain as day and rooted deep like an ancient oak tree.

Their apartment was too small to keep those kinds of secrets forever, and eventually the two of them abandoned their charade, although they never added any new details about why they ran away from Enceladus. They stuck to the same story. Her father had made many enemies, and after eliminating him, they would come for the rest of his family.

Jordan never seemed to care, but she didn't blame him. He barely remembered what their life was like in the dome, but she resented her mother, Imogen. Even if her father was never warm or particularly loving, he did what was best for all of them. He kept them safe and comfortable. He provided a life that neither Kasperi nor Imogen had given them since.

Her mother had given up not only her own life of privilege but also any chance Arabella and Jordan had to make something of themselves. It was an unfairness Arabella didn't easily let go of.

Her mother was an Armanic princess, but that was a title that meant nothing except to those deep on the ice and men like her father who believed in some old and noble history. The Solar Empire conquered the Armanic Federation and with their conquest buried their noble heritage forever.

Her father had been a noble. Hailing from a powerful house on Jupiter's moons, founded long ago during the Solar Empire. Except he was only one of many in his family. The Serras were numerous, and he was a minor son of a minor son. Still, clinging to their ancient history was how her father measured his own importance.

Arabella supposed marrying her mother had been his way to conquer like his ancient relatives and earn his own glory. When that failed to impress his family, he tried to earn it through business and failed at that as well. All his attempts for notoriety, as far as she was aware, left him empty-handed.

Maybe it wasn't his fault. They lived in a world with nothing to discover or take. The only thing left was the Republic and its pervasive decay and there was no one strong enough to conquer them. The Vermilion Coalition claims otherwise but they've hardly accomplished anything of note either.

In the years that followed their escape from Enceladus, Arabella was surprised to find out, by way of Kasperi's cousin Lena, that there was a bounty out for Imogen and Kasperi. They were accused of kidnaping her and Oliver, and someone had set a very healthy reward for their capture.

Arabella couldn't find out who set the bounty, but she assumed it was her father's family. All she could base that on was her knowledge of digiscreen dramas and how the noble families depicted were notorious for seeking revenge. They were also the only ones she knew with any kind of wealth to spend on frivolous things like bounties.

Mother had kept her and Jordan close in the first few years. Choosing to continue their education herself with what few books they had as teaching aids. They no longer had the funds for expensive Solite tutors from the Inner System. It worked well enough in the beginning, but they quickly outgrew what little she could offer.

To afford the luxury of more books, they needed more credits. Since Arabella was close to the age of majority during that time, it was easy for her to find odd jobs in shops and factories. Jordan meanwhile helped Mr. Chen make local deliveries from his store. All of them had to contribute, no matter their age.

Lena at least had been a big help in finding Kasperi work transporting shipments with their new vessel. The connection Arabella made with the bar owner's wife, Maggie, also proved useful. She was able to keep them busy with riskier but higher-paying jobs.

Most of the deliveries were local and involved shipping finished goods to neighboring districts. Then there were longer trips to neighboring moons and returning with raw materials to feed Titan's factories. Occasionally, a more mysterious job came through for the Vermilion Coalition. Those were the jobs from Maggie, and the ones Arabella looked forward to the most.

The Vermilion Coalition was an insurgent group that fought against the perceived injustice of the Republic. Most called them terrorists, but others saw them as their only chance of a better life. Arabella knew very little about them, besides that they paid very well, although that pay was commensurate with the danger of being caught working for them. Which was always death, typically a very violent one.

It was a big risk, but the rewards made their life much easier for a while. Schooling was also expensive, and if they wanted her or Jordan to ever have a chance at a comfortable life, they needed money. So Kasperi and Imogen didn't say no.

If the job required travel off moon, they would all go together so at least Kasperi could keep them safe. He never felt comfortable leaving them alone on Titan for long.

They had just returned from a typical trip hauling iron rods and broken mining equipment. Now, Arabella found herself walking toward Finn's, the same bar she had stumbled into so many years earlier.

Finn's Bar and Hostel was the local district watering hole and the source of their Coalition jobs. It was a small place, but always busy with local workers or traders passing through the nearby spaceport. Maggie was their main point of contact with the coalition.

To keep things secretive, Kasperi received the jobs through Finn at the bar. When Arabella turned fourteen and became an adult, she asked Kasperi to take over dealing with Finn. Her mother hated the idea, but Kasperi was supportive, and Imogen reluctantly agreed. It's why Arabella was going back there now to try and pick up a new delivery.

The streets were bustling. Arabella pushed and weaved through the crowds. The curses of disgruntled men and women no longer bothered her. She made her own space, which usually meant taking it from someone else. It was the way things worked in the lower districts.

The smells of dried meat, frying fish balls, exhaust fumes, and roasting nuts mingled in her nostrils. The smells made her hungry, and she stopped for a bag of roasted almonds drizzled with watered honey.

Nuts were one of the few foods that traveled well this deep into the Far Coast. These were a hardy variety grown on the moons of Jupiter. The premiere nuts were supposedly grown on Mars or Mercury. Apparently, they tasted much better, but she'd never had them and wouldn't have known the difference. The Jovian ones were still sweet and delicious to her. The rest of the way, she scooped them into her mouth from the oily bag, savoring the taste.

She pulled her jacket closed against the chill. It was a thin, heavily worn black jacket with faded patches. An old Pandora Fleet jacket that ended up in a second-hand surplus store. She was lucky to have gotten to it before someone else. It had cost her life savings, plus a little extra from Imogen and Kasperi, but it was worth it. It was her most prized possession.

She craned her neck over the heads of the crowd to find the best path. After a growth spurt, she already matched her mother's height at nearly six feet. Kasperi was still half a foot taller, but it was more than enough height to navigate the crowds far more easily.

The front of Finn's had a large neon sign that glowed brightly in the dim afternoon light. The windows were partially obscured by advertisements for cheap alcoholic beverages and lodging specials. Behind them, she could see the silhouettes of bodies moving around the bar and tables of the main dining room.

She opened the door, a bell chiming loudly to announce her presence. The main room was busy with a small group huddling around one of the tables. They were intently watching a game of Go. Among the group was a particularly fat man in a Mercurian headscarf that looked vaguely familiar. *Is that the man who sold us the new ship when we arrived on Titan?*

They were so engrossed in their game that none of them turned to see who the new arrival was, except for one eagle eyed man standing a few steps away. He was casually picking his teeth with a toothpick, his foot flat against the wall. He wore a long coat and a flat-brimmed hat that seemed out of place in the perpetually dark Far Coast.

What was most striking were his deep-set eyes. He wasn't physically imposing, barely more than average sized, but something about his gaze sent a shiver down her spine. By the time the door closed behind her, he had already looked away.

At the bar, several patrons, mostly working men and women in dirty coveralls sat drinking cheap beer from dirty glasses. Arabella approached a quiet side of the bar, and Finn came over to greet her.

He was roughly twice her age and normally youthful in appearance. His pale skin signaled his Armanic heritage, but he had no tattoos. The bags under his eyes seemed heavier than usual.

"Hey, Bella, welcome back. How was the last delivery?" he said amicably.

"Alright," she said, taking a seat. "You don't look so good. Are you sick?"

"I'm alright," he said, his eyes flicking behind her and back. "Busier in here than usual. Has me a little ragged." He set a glass of water down in front of her. The reusable plastic cup was scratched and stained, but the water inside was clear.

"How about a whisky?" she asked, eyeing the cup. She knew he kept a bottle of the good stuff stashed away under the bar. He had pulled it out the first time Kasperi came to meet him and Maggie.

Finn scrunched his brow as if thinking. "Are you going to pay for it?"

"Course not."

His tired eyes were momentarily brighter. "Best I can do is a beer, but this is the last time. In the future, you're gonna have to pay like everyone else."

He placed a pint glass of the cloudy, yellow beverage in front of her. She took a swig of the warm liquid, pinching her lips at the sour flavor. "What do you mean?"

Finn looked away, as if trying to come up with an answer.

Arabella pressed him. "What's going on, Finn? Where's Maggie?"

"She's off world right now," he said rather quickly and anxiously, "but you see that guy over there at the table?" He motioned with his chin.

She turned to look at the small crowd, purposefully avoiding eye contact with the eagle-eyed man. "The one whose back is turned?"

"No, behind him. The old guy in yellow and green."

The crowd momentarily parted, and she was able to see who he was talking about. His hair was pulled tightly back in a ponytail, and it was white from age. He wore brightly colored robes that complemented his tan skin. He was a Solite for sure. The longer she looked, the pieces began coming together.

He was a distinct and memorable man. His cane propped beside the table, its golden top shining brightly. She was right about who the fat man was. He was the agent of this old man from their arrival on Titan. She had thought a lot about him but never learned who he was. Until now, she had never seen him or the fat man again.

"Who is he?" she asked as if she knew nothing at all, which wasn't far from the truth.

"He goes by Mizraei. He's a trader from Mercury."

"What's he doing all the way out here? Can't he make more money in the Inner System?" she asked, turning back to Finn.

Finn shrugged, seeming agitated. He kept his voice low. "Maybe. That's what they say anyway. I'm sure he's got some reason for staying here. That's actually what I wanted to tell you."

"Tell me what? Why me?" she asked more defensively than she should have.

"Mizraei made me an offer for my place here," he said hesitantly. He was looking over her shoulder again. *Why does he keep doing that?*

"Like he's buying the bar? But you love this place. What about Maggie?"

Finn sighed and leaned in. Speaking sharply. "Look, it's more money than I've ever seen in my life. Maggie gets that. Besides, her logistics business is doing great. I plan on working for her." Arabella had never seen him so riled up.

"Alright, I get it. Are you leaving then? What about the jobs you've been getting us? How is that going to work. I don't know anything about that guy. We won't have to work with him, will we?" Arabella was immediately put off by the idea.

She could be happy for Finn if this was what he wanted. At the same time, the work Maggie got them through the Coalition was what kept her family afloat. Arabella didn't want to lose that.

"He's keeping me on for a while at least, so I'm not leaving right away," he said, his fidgeting intensifying. "The jobs should be okay though. Maggie was always the one with the connections. Me and the bar had very little to do with it. But we might need to start meeting somewhere else. Mizraei doesn't want anything to do with the Coalition, so it won't be here."

"But what about you?" she whispered. "You've been with them a long time, haven't you? Are you going to keep working with them?" She always thought Finn's bar was some kind of Vermilion Coalition establishment.

"Not so long really. I try to help where I can, but there isn't much a guy like me can do for them. I'm just trying to live my life too, you know."

Arabella didn't have any real loyalty to the Vermilion Coalition either, so she understood what he meant. For people like her they offered a way to make money and survive. For Finn, they were likely the same. They both benefited by doing the simple yet risky work the Coalition requested. Collecting and distributing cargo to the quiet corners of the solar system. The way she saw it, it was easy money, if they didn't get caught.

Arabella didn't mind if this meant she would be working with Maggie more directly. She liked Finn of course and cared about him after the kindness he showed her years earlier, but Maggie always seemed like the more responsible of the two.

She was about Finn's age and a rather tall and thin woman, even by Far Coast standards. Her features were plain and unmemorable, but she carried herself with confidence Arabella respected. Maggie always knew how to put Finn in his place and was a model for her own behavior.

The more she thought about it, the more excited she was by the idea of working with Maggie. It would be a great opportunity to learn and maybe build more of her own connections with the Coalition. Connections Arabella could use to be equally strong and successful, even if she didn't really believe in their mission. If it made their lives better, it was worth doing.

A shout came from the table where the large group was gathered. She looked back briefly at the noise, catching the man in the hat looking her way again, although maybe it was Finn he was looking at. The man turned away quickly, leaving Arabella uneasy. *Something doesn't feel right.*

Finn kept talking, oblivious to her discomfort. He was talking fast as if oxygen was in short supply. "Anyway, Maggie left me with one more job if you want it, but I think that's it until she gets back from her trip."

Arabella frowned. "When will she be back? You're making it sound like a long time."

Finn's face grew red, and he turned quickly to arrange bottles that didn't need arranging.

"I'm not sure, probably pretty soon. She wanted me to wait to tell you until she got back, but I didn't want you to miss the chance. It pays real good, ten times the normal rate."

"Ten times!" she shouted a bit too loudly. Regaining her composure, she added, "Why so much? Is it going to Pluto or the asteroid belt?" If it was, she knew they wouldn't be able to take it, even if it was a great payday. Their small ship wasn't large or reliable enough to risk such a long trip. "What's the catch?"

"No catch. They seem desperate to get the goods moving. It's going to Ymir, so not too far," Finn said.

Ymir was one of the small and forgotten moons of Saturn. It was deserted as far as she knew, but the money they were offering was nearly what they made in a year. If they did a good job, maybe they would get more jobs like it. Then they could earn enough money to get a nicer ship or maybe even a nicer apartment in a better district.

Arabella took a swig of the sour beer, trying to think of what to say. Her family entrusted her to collect the jobs for them, but they wanted routes to close and well-established ports, not faraway moons where they could end up lost and abandoned. She thought about the money and what it could do for them if they had it, feeling tired of struggling so much.

"Give me the contract. We'll take it," she said finally.

"Don't you want to talk it over with your parents? It's a quick turn, but you can go and find out before I give you the contract." Finn seemed suddenly hesitant, as if he didn't expect her to agree and now was second guessing something.

"You were saying it was important and time sensitive." His dismissive attitude only made her more obstinate. She placed her palms on the counter, leaning up to meet his face. "So, like I said, we'll take it."

He looked over her shoulder again. His voice breaking slightly, "Look, go talk to them, okay? The job will be here when you get back."

Was he planning to offer the job to someone else here instead? Maybe the eagle-eyed man. Was he offering it to her now so she would think he cared then apologize when she turned her back and someone else already accepted the contract? Finn had always been honest, but the industry was cutthroat. Either way, she wasn't going to let anyone else take something from her.

She slammed her fist on the counter to make her point crystal clear. "I *said* I'm taking it." She only vaguely registered the eyes that turned to study her.

"Alright, here," he said, pulling out a digipad from under the bar and held it out to her.

With the paperwork in front of her, Arabella paused, not to read the text but to consider if this was really a good idea. The job was outside their norm, and Kasperi would be angry she didn't consult him and Imogen first. But if she took it, he'd *have* to do it. It wasn't like their choices had been so great. They were barely getting by.

Arabella flicked through several pages of generic text before placing her hand on the surface, signing the documents. It wasn't like they'd had many problems before. This would go smoothly, and they'd be better off for it.

She then entered the information for their vessel into the manifest.

He took the device back from her. "Same as last time. I'll send this over, and someone will show up to load your ship. Everything will be cleared with the clerks."

She nodded her understanding and used her comm device to send a message ahead to Kasperi and Imogen. They replied quickly in confirmation and directed her to return right away.

Arabella downed the last of her beer and pushed the empty glass toward Finn. Imogen wouldn't like that she had been drinking, but she didn't care what her mother thought on the subject. She was an adult now and could make her own choice.

When she turned to leave, the hat-wearing man was staring at her again. This time, she was sure it was her he was eyeing. It reminded her of the spiders staring at her from the dark corners of their apartment. He broke his stare and stepped away from his perch to whisper something in the well-dressed man's ear.

Arabella said to Finn, "Who's the creepy guy who keeps staring at me?"

He flinched, quickly saying, "Don't know. Hired muscle, I guess. Never seen him before. Don't think he's said more than a few words the entire time he's been in here."

Finn didn't wait for her reply. Instead, he busied himself by serving drinks to the other patrons. One of those patrons, an older woman with a raspy voice, said, "Heard he's a bounty hunter from Luna. Tommy Buckley, they said. I've heard of him before."

"Sarding nonsense," said the man seated next to her. "You don't know 'em from yer own ass. He's another Solite tough guy hiding in the Far Coast, the kind that come here pretending they aren't washed-up nobodies. At most he's another Lunese pirate."

The two began to bicker about who knew what, but Arabella got the gist. The more people she met on Titan, the more she realized her old Mercurian teacher was right. No one from the Inner System lived this deep in the Far Coast by choice.

It was a place you ended up by accident of birth or as a last resort. That the man might be a bounty hunter made her nervous, but if he was from

Luna, she didn't expect him to know or suspect anything. Luna was a lifetime away.

"Thanks, Finn, I'll be back after the job. Hopefully you're still around for a while." Arabella gave him a weak smile. She would miss him if he wasn't.

"Yeah, I hope so," he said before returning to his work.

It hurt that he was being so casual about all this, but Arabella didn't linger any longer at the bar. She hadn't gotten any better with goodbyes during her time away from Enceladus.

Arabella made her way to the door, but before she opened it, a heavily accented voice called out. "Girl, come here. Yes, you by the door."

Tommy Buckley, or whoever, watched her as she turned back to the group, but he wasn't the one who spoke. Up close, his expression was even more frightening. The dark wells of his eyes bored into her. She had seen street thugs around Notus and in other dockyards on Titan, but this man was more intimidating.

Arabella considered bolting out the door, but her curiosity got the better of her. She approached the table. The old man in the colorful robes continued speaking, "Did Finn tell you who I am?" His long mustache fluttered with each word. He didn't wait for a reply. "I am the great Mizraei, new proprietor of this establishment."

"Yeah, he told me," she said flatly.

Mizraei ignored the game board while his opponent concentrated intently. Arabella only glanced at it quickly but didn't think Mizraei's opponent had a path to victory.

"What's a nice girl like you doing here anyway?" Mizraei said, appraising her. He wasn't leering at her, but she still felt uncomfortable by the questioning.

"Leaving," she said defensively.

Mizraei's opponent finally placed a stone with a sigh of relief and was countered by Mizraei, almost as an afterthought. "Stay a while. Do you play?"

"No, I only know the basic rules," she lied.

Arabella had spent plenty of time playing with Mr. Chen and routinely used those skills to separate cocky men like this from their credits, but she never hustled anyone in Notus. That activity was reserved for faraway spaceports they didn't visit too often.

Mizraei and his opponent exchanged several more turns before the game ended and the score was tallied. It was obvious to her that Mizraei had won quite easily, even without counting the stones.

The other man began to stammer, "P-please give me another game. One more!"

Mizraei shook his head. "Not how this works, Gerald. You know that."

Gerald became frantic in his pleading. The fat man struck him hard in the face. "You'll pay in credits or teeth. Your choice."

Arabella jumped. She wished she had already left, but her feet remained glued in place.

"H-how will my family eat?" the man said, rubbing his cheek.

Mizraei leaned back in his seat. "Maybe you should have considered that before you made your wager."

Arabella tried to steady her breathing. These were hard men who played by their own rules, not the law of the Republic. She knew the worst thing she could do was show she was afraid, even if she was.

Her mind went to the opportunities she could gain from an employer like Mizraei. Looking at his men, especially the fat one, it was easy to see they always had enough to eat. They also looked well dressed, and she assumed they didn't live in the squalor she had become used to.

Gerald only hesitated a moment longer before reaching into his pocket and holding out the credit chips. The fat man checked them for authenticity before tucking them away. He nodded to Mizraei, who waved Gerald away.

Buckley watched all of this with a steely gaze under his wide-brimmed hat. He looked pensive but didn't intervene.

"You think I'm cruel," Mizraei said, turning back to Arabella.

"The strong keep what's theirs. It's how the world works," she said, swallowing hard.

Mizraei seemed genuinely amused. "Sounds like an Armanic proverb. You're Armanic, aren't you?"

She nodded. "I was born on Pandora."

Most people from the Inner System like Mizraei assumed anyone pale and from the Far Coast was Armanic, an assumption that was seen as an insult by Jovians and native Saturnalians, who were culturally quite distinct. To be Armanic was to belong to a specific subset of people from the ice moons and distant corners of the Far Coast.

"Pandora, interesting. I've never been. Come play a game with old Mizraei."

She hesitated. The others were staring at her. She felt her comm device buzz in her pocket. Kasperi and Imogen were probably asking why she wasn't back yet. *When will they learn I'm not a child anymore?*

Arabella sat in the empty seat. "I don't have any money, but maybe if I win you can hire me."

"Hire you? To do what?" His smile was broad and jovial.

"You're a merchant, aren't you? I make deliveries. Always on time and not a thing goes missing," she said earnestly.

If Maggie left with Finn, they were going to need new clients. Even if things didn't fall through, more work was never bad. This was something she could arrange to show Kasperi and Imogen that she was capable of more if they let her handle things.

Mizraei placed his starting piece down on the board. The wrinkles of his face softening. Elders were rare, especially in the low districts. He was old, much older than anyone else she knew besides Mr. Chen. Except he had an energy that made him seem much younger.

"I saw you talking to Finn. He works for me now, and I don't work for the Coalition. Besides, I don't hire children."

"I'm not a child," she said forcefully. She hadn't been since she turned fourteen. "I'm looking to work and eat."

She placed her own starting piece, an uninspired and predictable novice move.

"I don't do charity. I'm a businessman."

"What if I beat you? Would you hire me then?" she said, looking him square in the eyes. The others behind him laughed.

His dark-brown eyes dug into her, and he didn't share in the others' mirth. "There might be a job you can help me with, but what do I get if you lose?"

"What do you want?" she asked, unsure what she could even offer.

He seemed to think for a long time. "How about a story? Your people are known for them, aren't they? Something noble and dramatic from your family history."

Arabella frowned. "Stories are worthless."

"Then why wouldn't you agree to share one? I've come all this way because I love the sights and culture of the Far Coast. The Armanic stories are the most entertaining of all."

He placed his next stone with little care.

She wondered if he was mocking her. "Would you make the same deal with a grown man?"

He smirked. "I would make the deal with anyone I thought had a story worth hearing. I'm something of a collector."

She clenched her jaw, but he seemed genuine enough. "Fine, I agree," she said, fully intending to win.

Her response elicited a raucous laugh from the onlookers, apart from Buckley who continued to watch quietly. Arabella turned back to make her next move.

CHAPTER

8

The game moved quickly, with each of them trying to establish board positions. In the beginning, Arabella would purposefully make a "mistake" or let time drag as she considered her next move, trying to reinforce the image of a novice player.

It wasn't uncommon for the poor to play Go, but it was exceedingly rare for them to be good at it. It was a game that required leisure time to play and master. Therefore, it was a game predominantly played by people from the higher social echelon.

She knew a man like Mizraei would assume she barely knew how to play and tried to play into that stereotype. In truth, she wasn't sure it mattered. He treated the game with such ambivalence that she would have thought he wanted to let her win, except for the fact that she was losing badly, and it wasn't entirely on purpose.

Arabella was forced to shift her strategy. Her moves became quicker and more purposeful.

Mizraei continued his lazy play style, matching her moves swiftly. He was good, very good. Maybe even better than Mr. Chen.

She placed her next stone with a shaky hand, brushing a loose strand of silvery brown hair from her face. She was making the most aggressive moves she could see.

A raspy voice said, "I thought you didn't know how to play."

She turned her head and saw it was Buckley. His menacing stare accelerated her heart rate. "I..."

"You're quite good for an ice rat," Mizraei said casually. "Were you a server maybe? Filling your master's cup and watching their games."

Her head snapped back to him. "I'm not a rat," she said angrily.

"Isn't everyone from Enceladus?"

"No! You take that back," she shouted before realizing what he said. Oh no. Maybe he hadn't noticed her slip. She could say she hadn't heard him properly.

She kept talking. "My father is a soldier. Finn can tell you."

Mizraei parted his hands. "Of course. He said something like that. I don't mean any offense." He placed another stone.

He thankfully dropped that line of questioning, and Arabella tried to focus on the board through her anger. She was still trying to find a way to win.

Mizraei filled the silence. "I'm excited to hear your tale. You can tell me all about life in that dome on the ice."

Arabella looked up sharply. Buckley was no longer leaning against the wall, and the fat man moved to block the doorway. *How does he know about the dome?* She thought back to the day they sold the transport, but that was nearly five years ago. Why did he show up here and now with these questions? She had to think quickly.

"I don't know what you're talking about. I told you that I didn't grow up on the ice or in any dome. I grew up in a small mining facility on Pandora. You can check my documents."

Mizraei placed his last stone, and she could see he had won. The way he raised an eyebrow implied he had won more than just the game. "I have, and the timing was quite...curious. It's why your story interests me. You aren't a normal ice rat or war brood for that matter."

She didn't know how much he knew, but it was obviously too much. The room felt like it was closing in on her. Heat rose in her cheeks, and she opened up her jacket, hoping to cool off.

"I need to go," she whimpered. "I- My parents are expecting me."

Mizraei smirked. "Of course, there's just one thing." He flicked his hand to Buckley who stepped forward. He yanked a single long hair from her head in a smooth motion.

She cringed at the unexpected pain and held a hand to her head. "What the sarding hell was that for?"

Buckley pulled a handheld device from his pocket. One she had never seen before. He pressed a button, and the machine ejected a small container. He placed the strand of hair inside and inserted it back into the device. A blue light began to flash as it performed some kind of function.

Buckley looked from her to the screen, and time seemed to stand still. She could have tried to run, but something kept her there. Arabella searched the black wells of his eyes for some sign of what was happening. There wasn't any hint or emotion at all. She turned to look for Finn, but he had his back turned.

Mizraei broke the silence. "Don't worry, girl. You might be scared, but the great Mizraei is doing you a favor. A leopard shouldn't be forced to live in the desert. It belongs with its own kind. None of this is your fault."

"I-I don't know what you're talking about," she repeated.

The light on the device changed to green, and Buckley nodded. Mizraei smiled. "Sure you do, Juliana, but I'm still very curious about your story. There's no rush, so you can stay a while and tell it to me."

"Maybe some other time. She's coming with me," Buckley said, and Mizraei's men adjusted their stance.

Maybe they weren't on the same side after all.

"We had an agreement," Mizraei said harshly.

"Yeah, and I have a contract with someone else that has its own stipulations." He pressed several buttons on his digipad. "My men are already collecting the others. When the deal is finished, your payment will arrive. Come on, girl. Let's go."

Arabella didn't move. She didn't want anything to do with either of these men.

Mizraei grabbed his cane and pointed it at Buckley. "I was the one who hired you. You aren't going to cut me out of this deal. She's staying with me until you collect the others and the bounty is paid. You wouldn't be any closer to finding them if it wasn't for me."

Arabella looked back again for Finn. This time he stood motionless at the bar, his eyes downcast. It didn't seem like he had any intention of helping her this time. The other patrons she realized had already left. Most people were smart enough to avoid conflict that had nothing to do with them.

"Their bounty is one of the highest in the entire system. You're out of your league, trader," Buckley said, moving his jacket to reveal a pair of pistols at his hips. Mizraei's men tensed and moved hands toward their own cudgels. Buckley smiled. It was the first emotion she had seen him show.

"Been a while since someone tried to test my patience. Go ahead. Make the first move."

The words weren't directed at Arabella, but she didn't need to be told twice. They were all ignoring her, maybe assuming she wasn't a threat. She used the opportunity to launch the Go board and its pieces into the air before darting for the rear door.

The men cursed, and Buckley tried to snatch her but missed. She made it quickly into the rear corridor, barreling past the stairs that led to the rented rooms above. The corridor was bright and inviting like she remembered. The colorful wallpaper on the walls was out of place in such an otherwise ordinary establishment.

A gunshot pinged off the wall where her head had been a second earlier, and she dropped to her knees. The door to the back alley was still several paces away.

Buckley called from behind her, "Come back, girl. I won't miss on purpose again. I don't want to hurt you."

Arabella wondered if he didn't want to or couldn't. Maybe he couldn't collect the bounty if she were dead. She had to make a choice. She sprang up and dove toward the rear exit. To her relief, another shot never came.

She made it into the alley. Her feet nearly slid out from under her on the slime covered walkway. There was only a moment to choose a direction. She ran toward the spaceport, knowing it was her only hope of getting out of here. Kasperi would know what to do next.

She could hear the curses and heavy breathing as Buckley and Mizraei's men tried to keep up.

She weaved through garbage and crates that choked the narrow alley system. Years of sneaking out of their tiny apartment was coming in handy. She turned left and then right, and then left again down an ever-growing maze of pipes, conduit, and trash. It got harder as she grew to navigate through these areas, but her slim build made it much easier for her than a group of fully grown and portly men.

She ran into a group of children deep in the warren of pipes and wires. They carried tools that looked to weigh more than they did. These were undesirable jobs that were often given to children who more easily fit in the tight spaces. She tossed the oldest child, a girl who was a little more than eight, a credit chip. "Hold up the men behind me if you can."

The girl looked at the credit chip with a wide grin and nodded. "Yes, ma'am."

Arabella continued, thankful for their assistance. The utility tunnels were also where people went to disappear. The children knew the tunnels best and could easily block a path before melding back into the scenery.

Arabella was breathing heavy. After a few minutes, she had to pause to catch her breath. Looking back, there was no sign that her pursuers were still with her. The children evidently did a good job redirecting them.

Arabella eventually exited out onto a busy side street. Dust-covered workers weren't unusual in this part of the city, so no one paid her special attention. She moved cautiously toward the spaceport to avoid attracting the eye of the Resident Watch. *You're another worker, that's all.*

The spaceport wasn't far now. Keeping her head down, she moved toward the side entrance. Her dread was growing with every step. She should have left the bar when she had the chance. *How could I be so stupid?*

She didn't know what Mizraei or the bounty hunter, Tommy Buckley, were capable of. Her only information came from digiscreen films that didn't share much resemblance with real life. Still, she was sure it wouldn't be anything good.

Approaching the spaceport entrance, she heard the first gunshots. *No, they couldn't have beat me back here.* That meant they had even more people working for them. That they had guns was more troubling. Only the military carried guns, especially after the Midnight Raids ended.

Even the most fearsome gangs weren't crazy enough to start a firefight out in the open during midday. If they were willing to risk a district purge, what weren't they willing to do?

She sprinted into the spaceport and toward where their ship was docked. The crack of gunfire echoed around her, but she didn't care. She could clearly see guards, military by their uniforms, shooting at an armored man. Their bullets bounced off his armor's shielding, which shimmered like light through broken glass.

Arabella dove behind a collection of crates to avoid detection. She crept behind the partial cover, keeping an eye on what was happening.

The armored man was Kasperi, wielding his old and battered lightning pike. He spun in practiced motions, stabbing and swiping at the soldiers who dared get in range, while charging others. A collection of bodies was gathering at his feet, but he seemed to be slowing down. There was still at least half a dozen more soldiers left. He was fending them off, but the rifle fire on his shielding was intensifying. It wasn't going to last.

Arabella grabbed a heavy wrench from a mechanic's cart. The tool was meant for detaching fuel lines. It was almost too heavy for her to wield, but she only needed to get one good hit with it.

Arabella crept up to the nearest soldier, who seemed hyper focused on Kasperi. The soldier wore no exoarmor and instead only had a ballistic vest and a light helmet. They were peacekeeping troops, equipped well enough to manage some local thugs but not to combat an armored knight.

She didn't hesitate, closing the distance between them. With a grunt, she hefted the heavy wrench and swung it around with all her might. It caught the man in the side of his face and chin. He dropped like a wet rag, but his fall attracted the attention of his friends. They opened fire, and she ducked back below the wall of crates and equipment as bullets ricocheted and pinged around her.

She grabbed the fallen man's rifle, avoiding the view of his crumpled face. The blood was pooling quickly around the weapon. She took it anyway, the warm blood coating her hands. She choked back the bile rising in her throat, trying to convince herself it was only motor oil.

Crawling on her stomach, she peeked around the side of the wall. Kasperi had used the distraction to his advantage. He was repositioned and pushing past one of the soldier's makeshift barriers.

Other dock workers huddled in the peripheries or inside whatever vessel was nearby when the fighting started. Arabella could see they were frightened and trying to avoid getting caught in the middle. More people were going to get hurt if they didn't get out of here soon.

Arabella glanced at their ship and saw Mother hiding inside with Jordan. They were huddled behind a collection of large crates that hadn't been there before she left to visit Finn's. She had to do something. Kasperi didn't have to fight for them alone.

Kasperi was living up to the reputation of the Jeevan on his face and the ferocity Armanics were known for, while her mother's hiding exemplified the weakness that relegated the Armanic people to their second-class status.

Arabella hated that her mother could sit back hiding instead of picking up a weapon to fight beside him. Imogen embraced her culture, but only as long as it was easy and demanded nothing from her. She wasn't surprised, but it inspired her to be better.

Arabella had never shot a rifle before, but she was excellent with her bow. Her aim came naturally with almost any projectile, from a ball to a rock. Kasperi had said a gun would be no different and explained to her how to fire one. All her lessons were conducted in secret to avoid her mother's intervention.

She looked at the bloody rifle in her hands. Her eyes drifted briefly to the face of its prior owner. His eye socket drooped toward his chin like a melting candle. It didn't seem like he was breathing, and she assumed he was already dead. Her mind only vaguely registered that information. It wasn't the time for second-guessing.

Arabella swung the rifle over the barrier and found her first target. A young woman, maybe not much older than her, who stood near the back of the spaceport. She was shooting from behind a metal support pillar. Arabella lined up the shot and fired. The trigger was more sensitive than she anticipated, and she fired several shots in quick succession. They peppered the area haphazardly, missing her target.

"Sarding hell," Arabella muttered. Checking the rifle, she adjusted the setting and lined up the next target. A middle-aged man about one hundred paces from the girl. She pulled the trigger again. This time, a single bullet fired as expected.

The man slumped immediately over the barrier of white vegetable sacks he was shooting from. Arabella stood transfixed as his blood began running over the white bags and thought of her bloody hands.

A whizzing sound echoed in her ear. Arabella was forced to dive back down for cover, finding herself beside the slumped figure of the first man she attacked.

Her thigh grazed his crumbled face, and she recoiled from the feeling. She kept expecting him to move. Instead, there was only one lifeless eye staring back at her. His mouth hung agape, cursing her with his final words. Arabella was paralyzed. Unable to move from behind the barrier or look away from the corpse.

She never noticed the gunfire had ended or that Kasperi had come to collect her. When he came around the side of the crate, she nearly unloaded what bullets remained in her rifle.

"Sarding hell, I..."

"Come on, there's no time. We need to leave. Now!" he said, half dragging her toward their ship.

Her mind was taken back to the day they escaped Enceladus. She didn't remember walking but felt the cold hard floor of the transport when Kasperi dropped her on it. The rifle fell from her hands and clattered on the metal.

Her mother swooped in to pick it up before she could gather her wits to grab it. "You won't ever need this again. You should have never picked it up in the first place," Imogen said harshly. Her brother Jordan was still clinging closely to her side.

Arabella felt her muscles tense and heat rising in her cheeks. She raised an accusing finger at her mother. "Me and that weapon saved you. If you didn't want me to hold a gun, then maybe you should have learned to fight yourself, instead of hiding behind Kasperi!"

He shouted from the cockpit, "Both of you, stop it. You need to take your seats. We aren't safe yet."

The engines fired up, and the ship shuddered enough that they both had to fight for balance. Imogen helped Jordan to a nearby jump seat, before placing the bloody weapon into a nearby lockbox like it was a piece of radioactive waste.

"There is more than one way to fight. I've raised you to be better than this."

The ship pitched dramatically, and they were both tossed into the adjacent wall. With a groan, she clambered to the nearby flight seat. Kasperi hadn't become a much better pilot in the last few years, but she felt like he had made the maneuver on purpose. Her mother regained the seat next to her.

"You don't need to put on a show for me, Juliana. You're still my daughter. I know you're tough, but you can be so much more than this. You don't need to be a killer," her mother said.

The use of her real name stoked her anger. "Unless you forgot, I'm only here at all because of you, but I don't care. I'll kill anyone who tries to hurt me or us a thousand times over. Kasperi would do the same. Any true Armanic would," she said defiantly. The soldier's crumpled face flashed in her memory, but she felt no remorse. It had been a shocking sight, but she knew it was necessary.

The ship banked hard again, and their bodies were pulled against their restraints. The noise of the engines was too loud for them to continue their argument, and Arabella was thankful for that.

She glanced at the large crates and containers strapped in the cargo hold. They seemed like any other shipment, but the crates bore a large crescent moon logo, which she knew represented Selenean Systems, one of the largest tech manufacturers in the solar system.

Luckily, the crates were already strapped down before they made their quick exit from Notus, or else they may have been crushed by the weight. Even worse, the shifting weight might have pried open the door or breached the hull and sucked them out of the craft entirely. That was always something you had to be wary of when transporting heavy loads.

Jordan sat opposite of her, clinging to the seat with his eyes closed. She wasn't sure if it was better or worse that he was too young to fully comprehend what was happening. Well, he was about the same age she was when they arrived at Titan. Maybe he understood a lot more than she imagined.

Finally, she turned to look at her mother. Her head was downturned beside her. Strands of silver hair, frazzled and out of place, clung around her face, but she didn't try to straighten them. She was staring into her hands as if looking for a secret buried in the veins and tendons that accentuated her skin.

The older Arabella got, the more she saw their similarities, both physically and in personality. She also began to separate her mother from Imogen the woman. She loved her mother, but she hated how easily Imogen disregarded her own heritage, choosing instead to be with a man like her father who would see their culture erased completely in favor of his own. Arabella hated her more for forcing the same fate onto her.

Kasperi chimed in over the ship's comms. "We're free of the lower atmosphere. Going to set a varied course for Ymir and make sure we aren't followed. Then we're going to need to have a talk."

Arabella threw her head back against the seat and stared up at the ceiling.

When the ship quieted to the normal low hum of engines and life support, her mother spoke softly, startling her. "Being Armanic isn't about being a brute or a killer."

"We fight, we fall, our tales are told," Arabella said, not bothering to speak softly. It was the most important Armanic proverb. They were words that needed to be spoken loudly.

Imogen sighed. "You're right. This is my fault as a mother. I didn't teach you the history properly, and now all you know is the version that was perverted and twisted by the Republic over centuries."

Arabella turned. This wasn't something she had ever heard her mother say. Not just that she was admitting fault but that the Republic had much to do with their history. "The Solar Empire destroyed the Armanic Federation. The Republic didn't even exist yet," she said, repeating what her mother had told her before.

Pre-Republic history was not a governmentally approved field of study. In fact, there were little to no records from that time in existence, beyond those explicitly approved by the Republic. Even then, most of those books were rare and valuable, especially if you didn't have access to a place like the Boundless Library. All of that meant that whatever she knew was from word of mouth, stories that were handed down generation after generation with varying degrees of accuracy.

Imogen turned her head to look at her. Brushing aside stray hairs. "That's true, but the story is deeper than that. I hoped to show you one day when we could return to my childhood home on Triton. There, buried deep in the ice, we have books that contain the secret histories of our people."

Arabella narrowed her eyes. Why hadn't her mother ever mentioned any of this before? Especially once they ran away from Enceladus or during the last five years when it became obvious they would never go back to the lives they knew.

"You're lying."

"I've seen them with my own eyes. My father took me down into one of the vaults and showed me. It was shortly before I left for Europa to marry your father."

As much as Arabella was intrigued, she scoffed, "Why would any of that matter? Even if it's true, they're only stories."

A cropped and bitter laugh escaped her mother's lips. "We fight, we fall, our tales are told. Didn't you just repeat that to me? You value the Jeevan on Kasperi's face, but now you tell me stories don't matter?"

Arabella bit the inside of her cheek. Her mother was right. The stories are almost all that mattered. "Well, what was in them then? What was so important?"

"I only had a few hours to read, but in that short time I discovered wondrous things. Most importantly, I learned that our people once ruled Mars, and it was the capital of our federation long before we ever set foot on the ice," her mother said, her eyes lighting up at the mere mention of it.

Arabella's own eyes went wide. That was truly something too amazing to be true. Of course, it was obvious that they had originated in the Inner System at some point. Earth was the original garden, but their culture never existed until they made their homes on the ice.

"Our homes are on the ice. It's a pillar of our lives."

Her mother smiled sadly. "It has become that, yes, but there was a time that our creations and culture rivaled the Solar Empire. It's why we eventually came to blows, and after a long and protracted war, all we were left with were the ice moons to call home. Here we've been ever since."

"You said the Republic perverted our history. It sounds more like the Empire are the ones to blame," she said, looking into her mother's eyes.

"I'm not a historian, but I can say this. Although the Armanic were always known for being fierce warriors, it wasn't until the rise of the Republic that they leaned heavily into that disposition. The Republic recruited our people to fight for them against the Empire and in the process separated them from their common history."

"You're saying the Republic used the Armanic people to win their war and then swept them back under the icy rug?" she said, trying to connect all the dots.

Imogen nodded. "Something like that, yes. It's why I was happy to support these missions when we made the connection with Maggie and the Coalition. If we ever want to retake our culture, we need to first break free of the Republic."

Arabella settled in to think about that. The Armanic people are deeply rooted in Republic military culture, and most are likewise extremely zealous in their devotion to God, even if what her mother said was true, and she had her doubts. It might not even be possible.

Kasperi came to join them after a time, and she was glad to see he was alright. He was still in his armor but had the helmet retracted. The exoarmor looked even worse for wear than it had years earlier. She didn't know how long armor was supposed to last, but this set seemed to be on its last legs.

"Autopilot is on for now. We should have some breathing room. Scans aren't picking up anyone tailing us," he said to Imogen before turning to Arabella. "What happened back there? We got the delivery from the Coalition, but then you never arrived. Those soldiers showed up and tried to seize our ship."

Arabella quickly thought of a plausible story. "I'm not sure. I accepted the job like normal, but then I was slow to leave Finn's. I didn't think it would be a big deal."

Her mother exhaled sharply. "When we agreed to let you handle the negotiations, it was with the understanding you would go and come right back. You could have been killed!"

"I sent a message that I was on my way. How was I supposed to know someone would try and rob us?" She left out any mention of Mizraei or the bounty hunter, not wanting to add another thing for them to criticize her over.

"You should have sent us a message before you took this job. The distance, the payment... It's far outside our norm," Kasperi said.

"Finn looked ready to give the job to someone else. I didn't want to lose the opportunity. We've been working for the Coalition for a long time. I didn't think it was a huge risk, and you can't say it isn't worth it," Arabella countered.

Kasperi clenched his jaw but didn't argue. Mother likewise remained quiet. They both knew it wouldn't have mattered if she asked. They wouldn't have said no.

"Someone must have known what the coalition was moving," Kasperi said, glancing over at the crates. "We need to get this dropped off as soon as possible. After that, we'll have enough credits to lie low for a while. Maybe we can go to Tethys or Rhea. It's good money, but not at the cost of our lives."

Arabella wanted to scream. He was suggesting they hide on yet another moon instead of carving out a life for themselves on their own terms. When mother agreed, she knew there was no use arguing, and she stalked off to the rear of the ship. She sat down, hidden behind a crate to stew in her own anger.

CHAPTER

9

Arabella

December, 4088 U.E.T. – Phoebe, Saturn

Although Saturn had an abundance of moons, most were small and far-flung places with few to no human inhabitants. Rumors suggested there was a time when any rock in the solar system with enough space for a transport ship to land on had some kind of human settlement, but that wasn't remotely true any longer.

Arabella sat in the copilot's seat beside Kasperi. She had her arms wrapped around her knees, which were drawn up to her chin. Her mother and brother were sleeping in the rear of the ship. A multitude of screens and lights flashed on the console as the dark moon of Phoebe came into view out of the small window of the cockpit.

The lack of human habitation and the great distances between places necessitated careful route planning around the few way stations that existed. In their case, that meant they would need to make a stop at the Saturnalian moon of Phoebe on their way toward Ymir and the outer edges of Saturn's orbit.

The trip from Titan to Ymir was substantially longer than their trip from Enceladus to Titan had been. That they needed to also take a more circuitous route, to avoid detection by anyone who might be pursuing them meant it was even longer still.

"We're approaching the Selenian station. We're going to dock, fuel, and be on our way. There won't be any time to leave and explore the moon," Kasperi said.

It had been weeks since they left Titan, and they hadn't prepared properly for the journey. They ate stale military rations for days, but at least they had a proper bathroom. Too bad the water system wasn't robust enough for them to shower regularly while still having enough recycled water to drink.

"I understand," she said, not caring very much for anything at this point. Her life had already been ruined for a second time, and she wasn't optimistic it would get better.

"You can get off and get us some food at least. We have enough credits to get whatever you want," he said before replying to the station's dock master via the comm system. They were getting instructions for the final approach.

"Food isn't going to put things back where they were," she said.

Kasperi opened his mouth several times, starting to speak and then stopping before trying again. Finally, he said, "If you want to talk about what happened…"

She knew that was an incredibly hard thing for him to mutter. Armanic warriors didn't comfort. They killed and told their stories but never showed remorse or sympathy.

"There's nothing to talk about. It's all part of my tale."

He breathed deeply, and Arabella thought he might have been relieved. Mother could say what she wanted, but Kasperi understood what it took to have a story worth telling. It took decisive action and sacrifice, facing danger and beating it.

She left the cockpit to change into a clean pair of gray pants and a faded-blue shirt. Her old Pandora Fleet jacket over top. Better they arrived without looking like Far Coast castaways. Jordan and Mother woke up when she began rustling through her things.

Their ship set down in the berth they were assigned by the dock master. Despite her initial apathy, she was anxious to get off the ship to stretch her legs.

The Selenian station was physically attached to the moon, along with a host of other buildings and tunnels that stretched out from its center like a less elegant spiderweb.

Phoebe had no atmosphere, although conspiracy theorists would have you believe every moon and asteroid once sported a perfectly terraformed landscape, all thanks to the Solar Empire.

If they were pushed to explain why there was no evidence of such a landscape, they would concede it would have been under an immense energy dome. If pushed, they would claim a relative dug up an ancient support pillar once on a utility repair job. If pushed further, the old pillar would magically become some fossilized plant and so on. It was all nonsense really.

Normally, the minimal gravity and the station's construction would have made her feel like she was still in interlunar space, but this station had gravity generators. The ancient machines were used to simulate Earth-standard gravity, which wasn't unusual for most way stations and similar facilities. At least those with working equipment.

The side passenger door of their ship hissed open, and she exited into a narrow corridor that led to another closed airlock. Kasperi, Mother, and Jordan followed close behind, as they waited for the next door to open. When it did, a customs official stood ready to greet them. He was a tall and thin Armanic man, maybe a little older than Kasperi.

"Papers," he said with a slightly annoyed expression. He had no guards with him and seemed anxious to be on his way when he saw Kasperi's Jeevan. "Sorry, sir. I'm in a hurry."

Arabella had experienced this same routine a hundred times over by now, but every time it still made her skin prickle and heart flutter.

Kasperi handed over their documents and said in Armanic, "You seem on edge, brother."

The man took the documents and began the normal task of logging them into his digipad. Their coming and going would be logged by the government for tax and security purposes. She assumed if his problem was with them that he wouldn't have come alone.

The man sighed, his face heavy with exhaustion. "Yeah, I wish everyone didn't always show up here all at once, especially when I'm the only official on duty for two more weeks." He continued going over their paperwork, stamping each booklet as necessary. Arabella was glad she had begun to learn the language and was able to make out the gist of what he was saying.

"It was pretty empty last time I came through here," Kasperi replied. "Is this normal since the Midnight Raids ended?"

The man shook his head. "The raids never touched us here. Usually it's pretty quiet, but we had a big corvette come through. Their crew's been cleaning the place out. We've got fuel for you, but not sure there's much else in the station beyond ration bars."

Arabella's stomach growled at the mention of food. She had been looking forward to finding something at least semi fresh to eat. "Nothing else on the whole moon?" she said in Standard. She didn't feel confident enough to use her Armanic.

The man frowned. Arabella was getting used to Armanics like him who found it incredibly insulting she didn't speak the language. "If you go outside the station, you could find more, but you'll need a shore permit."

Kasperi said, "That won't be needed. We have a tight deadline. Fuel and whatever rations you have will be fine. Is it a naval patrol that came through?"

The man switched back to Armanic. "Nah, navy doesn't patrol through here much. It's some Solite trader. Hopefully they'll be gone soon. The credits they spend are nice, but the paperwork is crippling." The clerk handed them back their documents along with a docking permit. "See the supply clerk down the corridor for fuel. The bar, food, and anything else is inside the main atrium."

Kasperi thanked him, and the clerk left them to their own devices. "I'll take care of the fuel, and then we can go to the atrium together. The ship isn't military, but we shouldn't linger."

Arabella wasn't as relieved but kept that feeling to herself. It was local dragoons that had attacked them back on Titan, so Kasperi and Imogen assumed it was the military that wanted them, likely because of their association with the Coalition. When they asked Arabella for more details about what had happened, she left out any mention of Buckley or Mizraei.

She was embarrassed to admit she might have made a mistake. She was also simultaneously hoping it was all some horrible misunderstanding. Even if those soldiers had been working for Buckley or Mizraei, what did it matter now? She didn't see any need to mention it when they were so far away from Titan.

Imogen said, "You both can stretch your legs out here or stay in the ship with me."

"Jordan can stay here with you, but let me go look. You heard the clerk. We can't leave if we wanted to without a permit," Arabella said, dismissing any of her lingering worries.

Even if someone was chasing them, they wouldn't know they were going to stop here. Why would she spend another minute in their smelly old ship if she didn't have to?

"I don't want to stay here," Jordan whined.

It looked like her mother wanted to object, but Kasperi gave her a look. "You can go if you take your brother, but I want you both back here in..." Imogen looked at her comm device. "Twenty minutes."

Arabella rolled her eyes. "Fine." She grabbed Jordan's hand. "Come on."

He came along without complaint. They walked down the narrow corridor toward a set of doors at the end of the hall. Jordan turned to wave at Mother before they passed through the airlock. When they exited on the other side, she let go of his hand. "Stay close to me and don't be annoying, okay?"

He nodded. "Do you think maybe they have any books here?"

"Did you already finish your last Milton Krane story?" she asked, a bit surprised. She had gotten him several new ones from the same store she bought her jacket. It wasn't very long ago.

"Yeah, it's been boring," he said, looking around absently.

There weren't many people in the corridor. It was much larger than the one that led to their berth, and she made a note of number 6-A on the door. Finding her bearings always took some time after getting somewhere new. Space had a funny way of disorienting you.

"Maybe they have some," she said, mostly to keep him quiet. She doubted they would have many books for kids here in the station, but she was impressed by how much he read at eight years old. He was a smart kid, much smarter than she was.

"Or maybe they'll have a Pandora Fleet jacket like yours I can get," he said hopefully.

Arabella started walking, following the signs that pointed toward the main atrium. "I don't think there are many soldiers your size."

Jordan wrapped his arms around his body. "It's cold in here though."

Arabella shook her head. He was probably faking it, but she had to admit it was a little colder than the stations they normally visited. His sweater was also made of a thin synthetic material that she knew wasn't very warm. "Why didn't you bring your coat?"

"I thought I'd be warm. Can we go back to get it?"

Arabella looked at her watch. It was a simple device with a pixelated display that only read the current time. "No, we don't have enough time for that." She exhaled and began taking off her jacket. Handing it to Jordan, she said, "Don't get it dirty, okay?"

The smile on his face softened her annoyance. The oversized coat hanging off his skinny limbs made him look like a cartoon character. "Maybe you'll get one that fits one day," she said, rustling his hair.

"When we're older, we can join the fleet together. We can be Falcon pilots!"

She smirked at the thought. Oh how their mother would hate that. "I'd like that, but first you need to grow, okay?"

They made it to the atrium, a large, vaulted room with a glass ceiling. If the glass wasn't clouded over with grime and dirt, making it mostly opaque, it might have been quite beautiful. She assumed it used to be.

In the center of the room was a circular bar that supported a couple dozen stools. Most of them were occupied, and there were three bartenders moving quickly to keep up with orders.

Surrounding the bar were tables where more men and women sat playing games like cards, dice, or Go. Others ate meals that were brought over by waiters from a nearby restaurant. It seemed like the only establishment selling hot food. Finally, along the walls were storefronts offering a variety of goods and services.

The tired expressions of the station staff echoed the clerk who greeted them. This was likely the busiest this station had been in a long time. When they stepped deeper into the room, they began receiving looks from the other patrons. Arabella realized her and Jordan were by far the youngest people in the room.

She also became very aware there weren't many other women. Instinctively, she moved to pull her jacket closed over her body, until she remembered Jordan had it. Instead, she put her head down and pulled Jordan toward one of the stores on the periphery of the large room.

"Let's try and find some food and hurry back," she said, trying not to sound as nervous as she was. Jordan didn't seem to notice anything was off.

They moved into a small shop that was empty of customers. The shopkeeper sat on a stool in the back absently reading a prayer book. He was a slim man with a balding head in plain clothes. He didn't seem Armanic.

He looked up from his book when they entered. "Welcome, new arrivals?" He spoke with a Jovian accent.

Arabella looked at him and then turned to look back at the atrium. Thankfully no one had followed them.

"Something wrong?" the shopkeeper said, looking behind her.

"No, nothing," she said dismissively. "Do you sell any fresh food here?" She looked around at the cluttered shelves of the shop. It reminded her of Mr. Chen's store back on Titan. There were plenty of supplies for cleaning and personal hygiene, but she didn't see much in the way of food.

"You need to go a little further down. Staying for long?" he said, indicating the shop he meant.

"Stopping to refuel."

"Better be careful not to linger if you're in a hurry. Might end up with a few marriage proposals. Pretty girls like you in a remote place like this aren't that common." He said it like she imagined a grandparent might.

She tightened her jaw, the back of her neck growing hot. "Thanks for the advice. Yeah, we aren't staying."

He smiled kindly. "Probably a good idea with this lot. Bunch of Lunese pirates. They're a bit rough around the edges."

The hair on her arms prickled, and she glanced around nervously.

Jordan found a container with some candy and pulled out several pieces. "Can we get these?"

"Yeah, whatever." She waved. "Lunese pirates? Are you sure they were Lunese?" Her mind went back to what the woman in the bar had said about Buckley. "Is that common out here?"

"More common since the Midnight Raids, but haven't seen or heard of any near here in a long time. They usually stick to the busier trade routes," he said, punching the amount of the candy into his register.

Arabella held out a credit chip. "Thanks."

"No problem. Fair travels."

When they exited the shop, her paranoia had reached a new level. She scanned every person in the room, looking for the eagle-eyed man or his wide-brimmed hat. Her breathing was fast, but she relaxed slightly when she didn't see him.

"You okay, Bella?" Jordan asked.

"Yeah, I have a headache," she lied. "Let's get to that other shop. Keep the candy in your pocket for later."

He looked disappointed but did as she asked.

CHAPTER
10

Arabella

December, 4088 U.E.T. – Phoebe, Saturn

The next shop was much like the last but with a Saturnalian owner who seemed more annoyed than happy to have new customers. His shelves were largely empty, but for a fellow Saturnalian he was willing to break out his secret stash. For three times the price, of course.

Arabella purchased a box full of noodles and crackers. Along with enough protein powder to last the rest of the trip. A packet of freeze-dried apples was the only sweet thing he had to offer. Fresh fruit and vegetables were what she wanted, but she bought it anyway. Something was better than nothing.

She hefted the box while Jordan carried smaller bags in either arm. The crowd was getting louder at the bar, but she gave it a wide berth. *Keep your eyes forward and make it back to the ship.* She got most of the way across the large atrium before a large man stepped in her path.

He was tall, maybe even taller than Kasperi. He had long black hair that hung loosely on his shoulders and wore a heavy cloak with some kind of fur on the shoulders. He smelled overwhelmingly of stale sweat.

She wrinkled her nose and tried to sidestep him without stopping. He moved to block her new trajectory. "Let me help you with those, beautiful," he said in a deep and rough Lunese accent. He loomed over her with his thick arms outstretched. He grinned, revealing a collection of mostly broken yellow teeth. She assumed it was from a history of brawls.

"We're fine," she said and tried to sidestep in the other direction, but another person, a short and stocky woman appeared to block that path.

95

The woman wore a long, heavy coat made of some canvas-like material. Underneath, Arabella could see the leather bands of gun holsters. "We won't hurt ya. Let us help get this stuff to yer ship." Her accent was even rougher than the man's, but Arabella didn't recognize it. Based on her dark skin and features, she was likely from somewhere else in the Inner System.

"I said we're fine," she said, sounding more panicked. She glanced at Jordan and saw him clinging tightly to the bags, his eyes wide and fearful.

"Everything okay here, miss?" a new voice called in Armanic. She looked to her right and saw a pair of young boys, maybe a little older than her, approaching.

They wore the uniforms of station security and carried simple wooden clubs at their hips. The boy who spoke had a comm device in his hand, probably what he would use to call for backup if necessary.

"Sard off, ice rat. We ain't talking to you," the man said, spitting in their direction.

The boy tensed, and Arabella hoped he wouldn't do anything stupid. This man could easily crush his skull in. "Let us go by, please," she said, hoping to appeal to his sense of decency. "We have nothing worth stealing. Here, you can even take our groceries."

"I'm going to call the heavies," the boy said to her in Armanic, and he raised the comm device to his mouth. She assumed he meant soldiers. She hoped he meant soldiers.

"Hey, drop it, kid," the man said, drawing a pistol from under his cloak. He motioned to Arabella. "You two are coming with us. Now."

If she dropped the crate, maybe they could run, but she had Jordan to think about. Could they both get away fast enough? His legs were shaking, and she worried he wouldn't be able to move at all. Sarding hell, why did these people want them?

Then she saw them. Leaving the restaurant in the distance were Buckley and Mizraei's lap dog, the fat Mercurian. They were waiting for them, but how did they know they would even come here?

The room had gone quiet. Everyone's attention was focused on the standoff. The cloaked man looked back to see Buckley approaching, and his smile grew. "I guess you know why we're here now. No point resisting. There's nowhere to go."

The security guard looked a shade paler with the gun pointed at him, but he did a good job of keeping a brave face.

"The sarding hell are you doing, Grant? Put that thing away. They're sarding children," Buckley said, motioning to the security guards in addition to Arabella and Jordan. "Now I know you don't want to, but both of you are coming with me. You already made me look silly once. We won't be doing that again."

The fat man said, "Mizraei will be pleased. Grab 'em and let's get out of here."

"How did you find us?" she said, trying to stall. She needed a plan and fast.

The guard boys seemed more confused. "Do you know these people?" their leader said in Armanic.

"Be on your way, boy," Buckley responded, also in Armanic. "There's nothing for you to see here. These two are with us."

"I'm okay," Arabella said while staring at the comm device. She needed them to leave so they could call for backup.

The Armanic boys took a step back. Why did Buckley have to know Armanic? She had to trust they would know what to do.

Grant lowered his gun as they did. "This is the only place between Titan and Ymir in this orbital path worth stopping at. It wasn't that hard."

Arabella felt even stupider that she didn't think they could have followed them. How did they know they were going to Ymir? Was their plan to steal the Coalition's cargo?

"We can give you the shipment. We won't fight you for it," she said, clutching at the box in her arms like a shield. It was heavy, but she found comfort in clinging to it, as if a cardboard box would do anything against bullets.

"You know we aren't here for some random boxes," Buckley said, appraising them both. "You can't hide the honey in your voice, the smooth skin on your faces, and the straight white teeth. You aren't ice rats. You're Jovians, at least in part, and you're far from home. I'm here to take you back to your family and away from the people who kidnapped you."

"Kidnapped?" she said incredulously. "Our mother is on that ship. I don't know who you think we are, but we aren't them."

Buckley paused, his eyes searching hers. "That so..." He adjusted his hat. "We'll have to take her too then. You won't have to live in this squalor much longer."

Grant said, "Let's stop wasting time, Buck. It's a long trip back to Luna, and we've been gone too long." He grabbed the crate from her arms and tossed it aside.

Arabella flinched, moving her hands up to guard her face. Jordan let out a scream and dashed in front of her, dropping the bags he was holding. Little fists held up in her defense.

When no hit came, she looked up and saw Buckley had stepped between them. He had his palm on Grant's chest and his other hand resting on the pistol at his hip. "Pick that up and apologize."

Arabella pulled Jordan close, seeing what he had done. A little boy standing up to a man five times his size. That he had the instinct to be so brave caught her off guard, but it made her proud to call him her brother. "It'll be okay," she whispered into his ear, even if she didn't feel it herself.

Grant matched Buckley's stare, and he looked ready to escalate the situation. The rustle of bodies and weapons behind him must have changed his mind.

"Sorry, boss, been a long trip, like I said."

The woman beside Grant said, "Yeah, boss, he didn't mean anything by it. We're just ready to get out of this shit station."

Arabella considered using their power struggle as a distraction to get away, but she'd have to carry Jordan this time, and she didn't think she'd be strong or fast enough to pull it off. So she stayed rooted in place.

Out of the corner of her eye, she saw the security guard activating his comm device. She assumed he was alerting the heavies, whoever they were. She thought maybe things were turning around.

When Grant backed off, Buckley stepped back, taking his hand off the gun. "Both of you, go find the parents. Take them alive."

Jordan cried out again, and Arabella tried to quiet him. Arabella was glad Grant was leaving. Kasperi could handle him, so she wasn't worried.

"Yeah, right away, boss," Grant drawled.

Arabella didn't get the sense he was happy to take orders. He also didn't seem to care about what Buckley wanted. Grant probably had friends who didn't like Buckley as much as he did, but they weren't in this room.

Buckley turned to Jordan, his features softening. "It'll be okay, kid. I won't hurt you."

"Let us go then. When we finish this job, we can pay you more then you're getting now," she said. "Please."

Buckley looked almost distressed. He glanced over at the fat Mercurian and then turned back to Arabella, shaking his head. "I wish I could do that for you, but I can't. I have a contract. You know how it is. In this line of work, you can't let every sob story get in your way. One broken contract and I'll never work again."

Arabella stared into his eyes, hope fading.

"I was hoping you weren't who Mizraei said you were. Honestly, I came here to steal his money. I didn't believe he'd found the long-lost Serra children, but the DNA doesn't lie." He reached over and plucked a long silvery hair from Jordan's head. "Best to verify both, you know."

The fat man laughed. "I told you the great Mizraei was never wrong."

"What if we don't want to go with you? Like I said, we're already with our family," she said.

"It's not up to you, kid, but I'd be happier if I were you. You could be lounging in some Jovian palace right now. It's not that great being poor or getting by on the scraps from others. I can tell you that much," Buckley said conversationally. He placed Jordan's hair into the machine and started it.

The mention of going back home filled Arabella with an odd feeling. It wasn't joy, but it also wasn't dread. It was a yearning to return things to the way they were, to pretend none of this had ever happened at all. To go back to the dome and climb into her old bed, dreaming of a world she still hadn't seen, a world she knew now didn't exist.

The chime of Buckley's machine caught her attention. She looked up to see his eyes narrow. She craned her neck for some indication of what the machine had revealed. Why did he have such an odd look on his face? Except he quickly stashed the device, drawing his weapon and grabbing

Arabella as a shield. She tried to shove Jordan away to get him to run, but he clung to her instead.

The source of Buckley's distress was a handful of men who entered the station. There were lightly armored soldiers wielding rifles with an exoarmor wearing knight at their head. The knight carried a lightning pike like Kasperi, and his armor was equally dented and battered.

All the faces she could see were clearly Armanic. They looked like proper soldiers who knew their business. This far away from any reinforcements, they needed to if they were going to defend against pirates.

The knight stepped forward, "Drop the children or your ship will never leave here, pirate."

Buckley held her tight and began taking slow steps backward toward his men. "The children are runaways. I have a writ for their capture. It bears the Duke of Jupiter's seal."

The knight's voice echoed through the speaker of his helmet. His soldiers kept their rifles raised. "A Lunese pirate with a Jovian writ. How unoriginal."

"Let me secure the kids and you can verify my documents. I have everything aboard my ship. I'm a bounty hunter, not a pirate," Buckley said, sounding a bit offended by the knight's accusation.

Arabella looked at the other members of Buckley's crew and didn't think she could tell the difference. With their hardened expressions, illegal weapons, and generally unkempt appearance, they certainly looked like pirates.

"Is that right? Are you a runaway?" the knight said in Armanic.

"No, he's a liar! My parents are on our ship," she shouted in Armanic.

"Sounds like you have the wrong person. Release her," the knight said, switching back to speaking Standard.

Buckley cursed under his breath. "I have a legal claim under the Fundamental Law of the Republic." His men, perhaps emboldened by that claim, brandished their weapons and took up defensive positions. "You have no right to detain us."

A stilted sound came from the knight's speaker, what she thought might have been a laugh. "The witness disputes your claim. If you can't provide proof of your writ here and now, I must insist you stand down."

After seeing Kasperi fight while fully armored, she knew this small group of unarmored pirates would be no match for this man. He would decimate them like a wrecking ball. Not to mention he wasn't alone.

"If I refuse?" Buckley said, his grip on her unwavering.

"Then we can fight for her and let God sort out the truth," the knight said, flexing his hand on the lightning pike. "Either way, your corvette will be forfeit."

That this man she didn't know was willing to fight so strongly for her lifted her spirit, even if it was his job. That Buckley had a corvette, a ship much larger and faster than their own, helped explain how they had beaten them here.

She had no idea what could stop such a large ship from leaving this station. She supposed it was like the movies and stations like these were more like miniature fortresses than simple space stations. Buckley's ship also wasn't a warship, as far as she knew.

Arabella tried to ensure this knight helped them. "His man threatened to kill me!" she said, pointing to the fat Mercurian.

"That so?" the knight said, stepping forward.

The Mercurian spoke in his own defense, but the knight wasn't listening. Buckley released his grasp reluctantly. Arabella dashed away, taking Jordan with her.

"Take your things and get to your ship, girl. The rest of you will remain here for questioning," the knight said.

While she was collecting the cardboard box, Buckley said, "You can't keep running forever."

She was determined to prove him wrong. They would deliver this cargo to the Coalition and collect their money. It would be more than enough to set them up somewhere new and beautiful. Maybe even in the Inner System. They could live a new life far away from this dark and lonely place.

Arabella ran with Jordan at her side. The contents of the box bouncing violently. They weren't being chased, but she couldn't shake the feeling that they were. When she found the right airlock, she slammed the door button with her shoulder, panting from the exertion. The door opened.

Oh no.

Kasperi was locked in place like a statue, the corpse of the woman who accompanied Grant at his feet. Arabella had forgotten all about them in her hurry to escape. Now Grant stood with their mother in his arms, a gun pressed to her head.

He was stepping back toward them to get away, but Arabella and Jordan stood blocking his path.

"Out of my way or she dies," he said, only slowing slightly.

"Mom!" Jordan yelled. Arabella was frozen, clinging to the box for stability.

"It's okay, kids. Go with Alfred," Imogen said, looking to Kasperi. Her eyes were wide and wild.

"Mom..." Arabella said as they got close. She couldn't get her legs to move.

"It's okay," her mother repeated, forcing a smile.

Jordan tried to run to her, but Arabella grabbed him when Grant tensed, pressing the gun closer to her head.

Kasperi regained some of his composure and motioned for them to hurry. She tried to block Jordan's view of the body as they passed. Up close, she could see Kasperi was panting but didn't think it was from the exertion of fighting the dead woman. Arabella could tell he was searching for a way to save Imogen.

Grant was nearing the airlock door with his hostage, all of them were powerless to stop him. Arabella considered reaching for the rifle that was stowed inside but didn't have enough time. If Kasperi tried to charge him, there was no chance Grant would keep their mother alive.

Even if they killed Grant...then what? There was already one dead body at their feet. Surely the knight who protected her wouldn't be able to do anything more. What if they arrested them for murder? If they let Grant get away, their mother would be safe, and the station guards would protect her. They could come back for her.

Arabella pushed Jordan into the ship and stopped beside Kasperi. Trying to will him to the ship. She saw how he looked at Imogen, their eyes locking. His gaze spoke of unfulfilled promises and a future that was slipping away.

"Get them out of here!" Imogen pleaded.

Kasperi growled, "We have to get her!"

Arabella pulled at him, begging him to stay with them. His pain tore Arabella's heart from her chest. There wasn't anything they could do, but how could she explain that in a single moment?

Kasperi stalled again, and Arabella felt like she was living an entire lifetime in that long moment. Her mother tried grabbing the airlock frame. She clawed wildly to stay with them. This was enough to break Kasperi. He charged, breaking free of her grip easily.

Arabella's vision narrowed, and the corridor constricted like her airway. Kasperi, Imogen, and Grant were on a collision course, and she didn't know how to stop it.

Kasperi charged, unarmed and unarmored. He may have well been naked for all it mattered. No amount of bravery would stop a well-aimed bullet from Grant's gun.

Arabella was suffocating. She needed to dislodge the obstruction. She ran to the ship to retrieve the rifle. Before she had the gun out of the locker, she heard the god-awful sound of gunfire. *Bang, bang, bang.*

She rushed back, rifle in hand, aiming it out the open door. Kasperi was on the ground, her mother nearby. They were both motionless, but their arms reached out for each other, their failing bodies fighting to fulfill the last wish of their souls. Their love was beautiful, but the sight of their bleeding bodies was unspeakable.

Grant grinned wickedly at her, his snarl echoing the evil that burned through him. He seemed to find glee in the killing, like a demon of scripture. Or maybe he found joy in avenging his own lost lover, sprawled out on the floor. He raised the pistol in his hand toward her. His thirst for blood or revenge hadn't been satiated.

"You sarding bastard," she shouted and raised the rifle.

Maybe Grant didn't notice she had the gun, or maybe he assumed she didn't know how to use it. It didn't matter, because guns and bullets didn't care who pulled the trigger.

His eyes widened, and he tried to back pedal but slipped on the bloody floor. He didn't make it to cover in time before her shots found their mark. Blood splattered on impact, coating the wall of the corridor.

She didn't wait to see him take his last breath. They would be coming for them. Either the knight and his soldiers or Buckley and the rest of his crew. They had to get away.

Arabella slammed the button to close the ship's door and ran to take the pilot's seat. She ignored Jordan's screams because there wasn't anything she could do about them now. She focused on getting the ship back on its way.

She was glad she had spent so much time in the copilot seat, learning from Kasperi. Luckily, the knowledge stuck, and she was able to get the ship in motion. She saw in one of the side cameras as the station's fuel hose snapped from the hull, sending fuel spraying. She silenced a multitude of alarms and flashing lights as the fuel gauge read less than half full before stabilizing.

It wasn't until they were far removed from the station that she finally exhaled. Her shoulders had been so tense that a sharp pain ran up her spine and neck when she tried to relax them, at least until she looked over her gauges again and saw the fuel levels were dropping faster than they should. When the station's hose disconnected, it must have damaged the fuel system.

"Sarding hell," she whispered, burying her face into her hands.

There was nothing that could be done about it now from inside the ship, and she had no equipment for a spacewalk, so she restarted the autopilot for Ymir and went back to check on Jordan.

At some point in their escape, his screaming had stopped, and he fell asleep from the stress and exertion. He was curled up in a ball, the over-sized Pandora Fleet coat held tightly under his chin. She grabbed a blanket and laid it gently over him. Hopefully he was dreaming of something nice.

Her mother and Kasperi were both dead in the blink of an eye. *No, I can't think about that now. We need to get to Ymir, to safety.*

Her mind and body numb, she returned to the pilot's chair and watched anxiously as the distance to their destination decreased only ever so slightly. They were moving too slowly.

She kept her eyes on the scanners. Buckley had already gotten ahead of them once. It wouldn't be long before he caught up to them again. Hopefully that knight would slow him down, but she knew his paperwork was probably legitimate. Her only hope was to make it to Ymir first and pray the Coalition could help them.

CHAPTER
11

Arabella

December, 4088 U.E.T. – Interlunar Space, Saturn

It was a painfully long trip to Ymir and a monumental struggle for Arabella to keep it together. Jordan oscillated between fits of frenzied crying and somber periods of clarity or maybe silent despair. She was having trouble keeping up.

They were both hurting, but she couldn't say it out loud. It had to stay buried away beneath the false confidence inspired by her father. Confidence that had no basis in objective fact. Jordan was counting on her now to hold it together, to salvage something from the catastrophe. He was looking to her for everything, and she had to grow up very quickly.

"It shouldn't be long now," she reassured him. "When we make it to Ymir, there'll be people who can help us."

Thankfully he had stopped asking if those people could save Mother and Kasperi. Neither one of them wanted to accept the truth, but they were dead and gone. And it was all her fault.

Jordan sat in the copilot's seat. It was the first time he ever sat in it. Arabella never let him before. He had the Pandora Fleet jacket zipped up and sat with his feet on the seat, knees drawn into the warmth of the jacket. His eyes were distant. "Why won't they leave us alone? Why wouldn't Mom and Kasperi let them take what they wanted?"

"Because they wanted us," she said, not for the first time. Having to answer these questions made her realize how horrible she had been with her mother. Arabella had put her in an impossible position with no good answers. She understood what that felt like now.

What she wanted to say was, "Because I messed up and led them right to us." If she had been honest about what happened back on Titan from the beginning...their mother and Kasperi would still be alive. She killed them as surely as Grant had, and the thought was eating at her. She hated her mother for how her actions led to the upending of their lives, but at least no one had died. What she did was so much worse.

Arabella looked over the navigation chart with a sigh. "Three more days." She left out that they didn't have enough fuel left to make the trip.

They would keep drifting of course, but they would lose power eventually. That meant they'd lose their life support and, even worse, wouldn't be able to stop. Even if they reached Ymir.

"Maybe they lost us for good," Jordan said.

She wasn't as optimistic. "Yeah, maybe." They were down to their last few gallons of potable water, so she flipped a switch to start a recirculation cycle. "Once the tank fills up, it's going to be the last fresh water. So don't use any unless you plan to drink it."

Jordan nodded.

Arabella checked the power reserves, and the ship indicated it wouldn't be enough to reach their destination. She wasn't sure what to do about it though. She wasn't an engineer or even a pilot. She had always made fun of Kasperi and his jerky flying, but it was far better than anything she could manage. Thankfully the autopilot was already programmed and kept them on course.

She tried to decrease their speed to see if it had an impact on the time estimate. Maybe reduced speed would cut the fuel load needed to stop. After a few minutes at the reduced speed, the numbers didn't change, and she cranked the speed back up to where it was. What she didn't realize was that there was a delay in the power output. It wasn't a Falcon but a slow and lumbering freight ship.

When the computer system finally finished cycling down and back up, it used much more power than if she hadn't done anything at all. Enough power that now the navigation system flashed red.

Jordan saw it and perked up in his seat. "What does that mean?"

She shut off the display, "Nothing important right now." The ship would keep a separate reserve for life support, so it wasn't an immediate issue. They would likely...probably, drift into Ymir's orbit before the life support gave out.

Then they would use the comms to signal whoever was supposed to collect the shipment. They were paying a substantial amount, so it was reasonable that whatever was in those crates was important enough to keep an eye out for. At least she hoped.

Jordan didn't press, instead he asked, "What are we gonna to do after we get to Ymir?"

It was a question she had been thinking about quite a bit. "Go somewhere far away from here."

"Like Europa? Where Dad was from?"

"Hopefully even further," she said, looking at him. One day she would tell him their father's family was the reason they had to run. His goons were the reason Mother and Kasperi were dead. They couldn't go back to them now. "Somewhere you can see the sun in the sky, as big as Saturn. It shines so bright you can't even look at it without going blind."

"As big as Saturn?" his voice was full of wonder. They both remembered the first time they saw its mighty rings on the ice. The planet was so bright it blocked out all the stars except for the tiny speck of the Sun. "There's no way it can be that big. It would burn us up."

She laughed. "You're probably right. Maybe it's not that big, but it's still much bigger than you."

He grimaced. "I'll get taller! Maybe we could go to Luna, like Dad said, remember?"

She thought of Buckley and his Lunese crew, but then she also considered the large Armanic population that supposedly lived there.

"Maybe," she said, hoping they would live long enough to even make the choice of where to go next.

○

Two days later, Arabella was watching Jordan reread one of his old books when the ship's alarm began to blare. The book's spine was worn and creased from repeated reading. She didn't know why, but it made her sad and angry that she never got him a new one.

She was so angry that it took her a long time to register what was happening. They had run out of fuel earlier than she calculated. The engines died, and everything became eerily quiet.

Jordan put down his book when the lights dimmed to emergency energy save mode. "What happened?"

Arabella swallowed. There was no sugar coating it. "We're out of fuel."

"How... How will we make it back?" Panic was rising in Jordan's voice.

"We're still moving in the right direction."

"But we won't be able to stop," he said, and she wished he wasn't so smart.

"Someone will catch us before that happens. The Coalition is looking for us," she pressed several buttons to stop the alarm. Then she eyed the emergency beacon.

"What is it?" he asked, noticing her change in focus.

"I'm thinking of something. Here, you can use this to keep reading." She handed him a small flashlight from the emergency kit under the console.

He took it reluctantly and sat back down in the copilot's seat.

Pressing that button would give them the best chance of survival. It would also make it easy for Buckley to find them if he was still looking. Maybe it was better than the unknown or trying to scrape by on her own.

There was also the chance no one was listening at all. If no one came they would continue drifting out into space until eventually running out of air or food. She figured they were going too fast for Ymir's gravity to trap them. She tried not to think of that.

Long after Jordan left the cockpit to sleep, she was still staring at that cursed button. She didn't want to accept reality.

I have to press it. It's our only chance.

She lowered her head in a silent prayer. Not only to God but to her mother and Kasperi. To any of her ancestors who were listening. Even to lost spirits that might take pity on them.

With one long breath, she moved her shaky hand. She opened the button's protective lid with one hand while brushing hair from her face with the other.

"There won't be anyone to tell our tales if we die here," she said softly. "I'm sorry I wasn't honest. I never thought any of this could happen." She spoke into the void, hoping her voice might find Mother and Kasperi's ears. "But I swear I'll avenge you both. Your tales *will* be told."

She pressed her palm down on the red button. The digiscreen display lit up briefly to note their emergency signal was broadcasting before going dark once again. Their fate was in God's hands now.

○

There was nothing left for them to do but wait. Another day went by. Based on the original estimate from the nav system, they should have been within range of Ymir's orbit. Except nothing happened. No rescue ship came to scoop them up. Even Buckley didn't appear to steal them away to some other fate. Whatever it was would be better than dying in space.

Instead, there was more darkness and more nothing. The backup power supply was now dangerously low. Without it, the life support systems would cease to function, and then eventually the oxygen in the ship would run out as they replaced it with carbon dioxide.

Unable to wait any longer, she decided to turn the consoles back on to check their position. When the digiscreens hummed to life, Jordan was roused from his sleep in the cargo compartment.

"Did we make it?" he called excitedly.

The ship was getting cold after so long without the engines running. The emergency heaters were hardly sufficient. His breath hung in the air as he spoke, and he wrapped himself in a blanket.

Arabella hesitated before answering and her heart sank when she saw the navigation screen. They were sailing past Ymir, and fast. Without power, they had no way to slow their approach, and now it was too late. She fell heavily back into the pilot's chair.

"No," she said, her voice cold as ice.

Jordan came close, sensing her despair. He stood beside her and buried his face in her shoulder.

She wrapped an arm around his small body and whispered, "I'm sorry. I tried. I'm sorry for everything."

"It isn't your fault," he said adamantly.

It hurt because she knew he was wrong, even if he really believed it.

"No, I need to tell you something," she said, pulling him off her shoulder. She was going to tell him everything, even if he wouldn't understand. She owed him the truth. It would be her last confession before God and her ancestors, with her brother as a witness.

"What is it, Bella?"

"Everything that happened, all of this," she began to speak but paused when a heavy thud resounded in the cabin.

They both looked around for the source of the noise.

"Was that a rock?" Jordan asked, his nose scrunched.

It wasn't unusual to deal with small space debris, but then there was a second thud. "I... I don't think so." The noise was much louder than a small rock. The interior of the ship began to rattle, but she didn't understand what was happening.

There was no other warning before their ship lurched and suddenly fell into a gravity well. Their bodies remained in motion, and they were both tossed violently into the control console. Arabella saw Jordan fly headfirst into the display. He went limp on contact. Meanwhile, she smashed her hip and side, excruciating pain radiating up her chest and down her leg.

She landed roughly on the floor, almost getting wedged between the pilot's seat and the controls. She crawled over to Jordan, who was bleeding from a large cut on his scalp but still breathing. Thank God.

"Jordan! Can you hear me? Jordan!"

A quick glance at the controls showed they weren't moving anymore. Someone had finally found them.

CHAPTER

12

Arabella

December, 4088 U.E.T. – Ymir, Saturn

She checked the viewing ports, but without the cameras it was hard to make out anything useful. Something had grabbed them, that much she was sure. It was the only explanation for why they weren't moving.

She sat on the floor in the cargo area, cradling Jordan in her arms. "Jordi...please. You have to wake up."

"What... Mom?"

"Jordi, it's Bella. You're safe. It's going to be okay."

"My head hurts," he gasped but didn't open his eyes.

"It's okay. It's going to feel better soon." She fought back the forming tears. She had to stay strong. She couldn't lose him too.

The ship shook again, and it sounded like they landed on something. It wasn't long before she heard an aggressive knocking on the hull and muffled voices. She ignored them. Another knock followed, and when she didn't respond, torches began cutting through the side hatch.

Arabella continued to rock Jordan back and forth in her arms. She could feel the warm blood from his wound against her chest and soaking into her shirt. She grabbed a rag to try and staunch the bleeding.

How could such a small body have so much blood?

The torches howled, and smoke poured into the cargo hold. Molten metal dripped near her feet. Shuffling back from the door, she tried to keep pressure on Jordan's head. Her body was shaking, and she couldn't really feel her legs.

She could see light creeping through where the torch cut, and a sinking feeling washed over her. There was no guarantee this was salvation. She set down Jordan long enough to retrieve the rifle from the locker. Checking the ammunition, she saw there wasn't much left. Slinging the strap of the weapon over her shoulder, she went back to Jordan.

The door eventually peeled away and slammed loudly onto the ground outside. Well, not ground but the inside of a hangar bay. It was clearly a ship much larger than their own.

A soldier with a flashlight approached and shined it into the cargo hold, stopping to hold it over Arabella and Jordan. She raised her hand to block the light.

He shouted something she didn't hear or understand.

"Please...help my brother."

The man shouted back, but she couldn't see him well through the bright glare of the light.

Arabella stood up on numb, shaky legs, Jordan in her arms, the rifle hanging close to her side. He was almost too big for her to carry, and her legs threatened to buckle. Years of carrying cargo were the only thing that kept her upright.

Approaching the door, she saw the man had a rifle trained on her. Arabella adjusted as best she could to grab her own gun.

She limped into the hangar bay and shouted again, "Please, my brother is hurt! I need help!"

The hangar bay was large enough to accommodate her ship and then some. A half dozen or more faces were arrayed around her. Some looked like soldiers, while others looked like regular sailors.

"Sarding hell..." A low, familiar voice came from somewhere in the back of the crowd. Buckley and his familiar hat stepped forward.

Arabella knew deep down inside it would be him. Hoped it wouldn't be but *knew* it would. God or something wanted her to live this moment, to face the challenge or drown in the attempt. She was ready to strangle him then and there.

"You... You killed them."

Buckley spoke sharply to a man next to him. "Go, get Sofia. Don't just gawk at me, hurry!"

"Don't pretend to care now," she said, trying to brandish the gun at him. "Or is it because we're worth less dead?"

He shook his head, his palms held out. "I told you from the beginning I only wanted to take you both home. That you're worthless dead is obvious. Still, I'm not in the business of killing kids."

"That monster Grant didn't seem to mind. You sent him to kill my mother," she growled, snot and tears mixing on her face.

"You heard me tell him not to. That was never the plan. Grant is... was a liability. That Armanic knight of yours did me a favor getting rid of him."

"His name was Kasperi!" she yelled, trying to step forward. She didn't correct him that she was the one who killed Grant. Her legs wobbled. She felt something inside her leg and hip buckle, and a sharp pain radiated through her body. She collapsed instantly.

It took all her strength to make sure she didn't drop Jordan. She set him down gently and took the rifle in her hands, raising it up threateningly. Protecting him was the only thought she had space for in her mind.

"You have to save him..."

The soldier beside the ship stepped forward, a jovial laugh on his lips. He thought this was all a joke, that she wasn't a threat. She pulled the trigger, firing a single shot. It hit him in the chest. He collapsed to the ground, the smile glued to his face. Dead.

She felt no remorse. She was never going to be a victim again. None of these people were going to get the best of her. Her story to tell would be one of victory and honor.

The room went quiet, except for the sound of rustling weapons. She looked back to see at least a half-dozen guns trained on her. She raised the rifle at Buckley.

"You're going to save him."

He held his hands up. "Put the gun down and we can do that."

She didn't comply. If Buckley wanted them alive, this was the last card she had to play. Another one of his goons crept forward as if to grab her. She shot him too, but this time her aim wasn't spot on. The man fell cursing on the ground, clutching at his leg. Good enough.

"Anyone else?" Hopefully they got the message, because she didn't have much ammo left. They might be assuming the same thing.

An older woman carrying a bag with a large white cross on it came running in a moment later. She had her hair tied back in a ponytail and seemed more put together than the others.

Seeing Arabella, she stopped in her tracks, raising her hands like Buckley. Arabella nodded, and the woman began walking to the writhing man with the leg wound.

Buckley interjected, "The boy, Sofia."

Sofia stopped to quickly scan the room, and her eyes widened like she hadn't noticed Jordan there originally. She rushed over to kneel beside him, suddenly disinterested in the gun.

Arabella said, "You have to save him."

"What happened to him?" Sofia sounded like the hospitaller they went to see in the dome as kids. The physician that would give them medicine when they were sick or bandage their scrapes and cuts.

"I don't know. He's bleeding so much."

Sofia leaned in with an ear to his chest and mouth. "He's still breathing. That's good."

"The bitch shot me, and you're helping them," cried the man with the bullet in his leg. He seemed to be as angry as he was in pain.

"Did I tell you to move? That's your own sarding fault," Buckley snapped. Arabella wondered if he was mad the man wasn't following orders or if he cared about them like he claimed.

"I need to take him back to the medical room," Sofia said, finishing her quick exam.

Arabella adjusted the gun. Her breath was shallow and strained. Her head was swimming. "You can help him here."

Sofia stared, her face a mask of calm. "If he stays here, he'll die. There's swelling I need to release. I can't do that here safely. He'll die from an infection quickly enough if I operate on a hangar bay floor."

Her little brother couldn't be operated on in some random ship, alone and far from home. "Alright, I'm coming with you. Only us, no one else."

"I can't allow that, not while you're holding that rifle. Put it down and we can talk," Buckley said, his hand resting on his pistol. She never saw him reach for it.

Arabella pointed the gun at him, and they were locked in that moment. His eyes weren't cold or menacing. She noticed they were darting between herself and Sofia. Whoever she was, she was important to him. He probably wanted to keep her safe. "You can come too, but that's it."

Buckley nodded slowly. "That's a start. I promise I'm not your enemy."

She wanted to believe him. She wanted so badly for all of this to be over, for all of it to have meant something more than the random death of her mother and Kasperi. Most of all, she wanted Jordan to be safe and happy, even if she could never be.

Before she could answer, an alarm chimed, followed by red flashing lights. She didn't know what they meant but assumed it was nothing good when the crew began looking frantically at each other.

Buckley activated his comm device and cursed at whatever news he received. "Everyone, man your stations. We've got company."

In the confusion, she noticed a woman in the corner of the room she hadn't seen before. She was crouched behind a stack of crates, a rifle resting on her arm. She had it aimed right at Arabella. Buckley was trying to distract her.

Arabella redirected her aim and fired several shots. Hoping at least one would hit its mark.

Unexpectedly for all of them, the ship shook violently, knocking nearly everyone from their feet. Thankfully she was already on the ground.

Sofia clung to Jordan, and she decided the woman would be able to care for him best while she defended herself. Arabella tried to get to her feet, but her hips and leg were stiff and swollen. They were totally numb and refused to move. She was stuck like a turtle on its back. She crouched behind Sofia, hoping Buckley's men wouldn't risk shooting at her.

Bullets began to ping around her, and she knew she made the right choice.

Buckley shouted at them to stand down, and they did. At least until the hull of the ship itself began to melt. It was one thing to burn through the door of a small transport ship. It was something very different to burn a hole through the thick hull of a large starship.

They turned, readying their guns for the new threat, so they weren't prepared for the storm that came from elsewhere through the main corridor.

Armored soldiers appeared from the corridor while the hull burned. They fired on the pirates. Buckley rushed over to where she sat with Sofia. Arabella turned her rifle on him, pulling the trigger, but nothing happened. She was out of ammo.

"So much for thanks," Buckley said, pulling on Sofia's arm. "We need to go, *now*."

His men were severely outmatched by the new arrivals. Buckley unloaded his pistol on one who came too close, while his men provided supporting fire. The knights armor began to overheat, and he was forced to retreat. Buckley's men were holding, but it was like trying to stop a pride of lions with a flyswatter.

Arabella grabbed for Jordan, but Sofia pulled him away. "There's no time. Come on." The woman stood up, carrying his limp body. Arabella tried to stand and follow, but her legs wouldn't work. She fell roughly back down to the floor. Pain radiated up her side, and she cried out.

Buckley came back to take her by the arm. "I got you, kid."

She screamed in agony. It felt like someone was dragging a hot knife up her side. The heat exploded from her hip, and she couldn't stand, even on what she thought was her good leg.

He struggled to hold her up with one arm while firing at the soldiers with his other. She didn't know why he was helping her or who the new arrivals were. Maybe they were with the Coalition, but they could have also been Republic soldiers. Jordan was gone, and she had to follow him.

Arabella clung to Buckley with whatever strength she had left, letting the rifle hang limply from the strap on her shoulder. It was useless now anyway without any ammunition. One of Buckley's men rushed over to help, taking her other arm. They made some progress toward the rear hangar door, but then the metal from the hull crashed, and the breach was made.

A metal cannister flew inside through the smoking maw. It hit the metal floor of the hangar with a clang and rolled toward them in slow motion. Her dread rose as nothing happened until there was a sharp blast, followed by a wave of pressure and a blinding light.

She was dropped by the hands that held her, and she fell to the ground with a new wave of pain. Her eyes only saw white, and she fumbled for help. She tried to yell, but her ears rang so badly she wasn't sure any sound came out at all.

A heavy hand tried to grab her. It was an armored hand. Like when Kasperi had scooped her off the ice to safety, except this hand wasn't gentle. All the movement was making her injury worse, and she lashed out instinctively. Grabbing the rifle that was still strapped to her back, she swung it wildly, feeling the reverberation through her hands as she hit something hard.

She didn't stop swinging until her vision began to clear and she could see no one was trying to grab her. The smoke dissipated, revealing a trio of armor-clad knights standing guard over her. Their armor was black, save for a blue and gold insignia on the shoulder, depicting a swirling black cloud. On closer inspection it looked like the event horizon of a black hole. More soldiers in black exoarmor poured out of the molten opening like roaches from a drain.

Arabella was panting, unable to move and unable to fight. Buckley's men were dead or gone. Buckley and Sofia were likewise nowhere to be seen. He had abandoned her too.

Arabella cried out in panic. "Who are you? I need to find my brother. You need to save him!"

The soldiers stood like owls, their bodies rigid, while their heads swiveled in search of prey. They didn't answer her question. Their eyes and faces hidden behind silver visors.

She slammed the rifle against the ground in frustration. "Why won't you answer me?" She flung the useless weapon at the nearest soldier. He must have thought it wouldn't reach him, because he didn't move, and it struck him in the leg. The shielding of his armor shimmered briefly, and she thought she heard muffled laughs from inside their helmets.

She had never seen so many armored knights in one place, especially knights with such beautiful armor. Her father had new armor, but it hardly looked this expensive or capable. His was more of an art piece than functional equipment.

These men and women looked like they knew their business as well as Kasperi but somehow also had enough money to fund their enterprise.

One of those armor sets alone would be enough to feed a small low district for a lifetime.

When they didn't answer, she began crawling toward the rear exit, the one Sofia had been heading for with Jordan. They didn't try to stop her, but she was a slug trying to cross hot concrete. Each movement was agonizing and slowly killing her.

"You are a testament to your people, child."

Arabella turned to see a tall woman approaching. Her armor was similar, except it was adorned with blue inlays. Notably at her hip was the heavily jeweled hilt of a plasma blade. Arabella had never seen one in real life, but she would recognize one anywhere from the digiscreen shows.

When she got closer, the woman retracted her helmet. She had unblemished, pale-olive skin. Her hair was light brown, almost auburn, and was tied in a single long braid. Most striking of all were her brilliantly emerald eyes.

Arabella stared, trying to figure out what was going on. The woman looked familiar, but she didn't know why.

"Do you know who I am?" she asked, kneeling beside Arabella. She was graceful, and up close her armor looked even finer.

Arabella stared at the hilt of the plasma blade. It sparkled brilliantly, and if the armor had cost enough to feed a low district, that one blade could feed all of Enceladus for a lifetime.

Whoever she was, she was important, and so Arabella averted her eyes, bowing her head as much as she could in her crippled state.

The woman placed a hand softly on her chin and forced her to look. "I'm not a god, only a woman."

"I'm sorry, Milady. I don't know who you are, but they took my brother. I need to find him. You have to help me."

Arabella blanched, realizing what she said. The thought of ordering a woman like her to do anything was ludicrous, but she was acting on pure instinct. Her sense of propriety had died a long time ago with Juliana anyway.

The woman smirked. "You are much older, but you remind me of my daughter. Bold and assertive." She released Arabella's chin. "We have taken control of the ship. Several life rafts escaped, but we will find them. If your brother is among them, we will find him too. What's your name child?"

"Arabella Smith. Please, you need to help."

The woman's face remained neutral, and she spoke in a slightly odd accent. "My name is Semiramis al Vardan, Grand Marshal of the Void Knights. Do you know who they are?"

Arabella's eyes went wide in recognition. She remembered now where she had seen her face. It was on the digiscreen standing behind the Republic's supreme leaders, the Vox and Manus at parades and speeches in the Capital on Mars. Seeing her outside of a palace and armored didn't fit with what she knew of the woman.

"You... You're the Duchess of Mercury," she said in disbelief. That title was far more interesting to her than thinking of her as some stuffy judge.

There were eight knightly orders, one for each planet and its moons. They served to control the courts as seneschals and judges on behalf of the clergy, like the Knights of the Aether that controlled the Saturnalian system. Then there were the Knights of the Void, who had jurisdiction over all of them.

"Yes, but I'm here in service to my knightly order. Is this your vessel?" she asked, motioning to the heavily damaged transport ship.

Arabella was about to say yes when she thought of the Coalition cargo in the back. She didn't know what was in the crates but worried it would be something she couldn't explain to the authorities.

"No. Well..." She considered the ship was registered to Kasperi or her mother and could be traced back to them. "It was my mother and father's. My brother and I came with them for a delivery, since it was a long trip." Lady Vardan wouldn't know it was her biometrics on the contract, would she?

The wry smile on the corner of the woman's lips was a bad sign. "You really do remind me of my daughter. Are you injured? We will take you back to my ship, and there we can speak further."

"I *need* to find my brother," she reiterated.

Lady Vardan stood back and held her arm out. "Lead the way."

Her cheeks warmed, and she looked up at them. "I... I can't walk."

Arabella was thankful when the older woman didn't laugh. "You have done everything you can, child. Now it's up to us. We will bring the pirates responsible for this to justice."

She didn't trust this woman. Lady Vardan was an agent of the government, and Arabella's experience with people from Mercury was less than promising.

For some reason, the woman continued to talk to her, maybe because she wanted information about the Coalition. Arabella didn't know for sure but knew she didn't have much choice. Where else was she going to go? Who else would help her?

Lady Vardan motioned for one of the soldiers to pick her up.

This time, the armored hands were gentle. She winced involuntarily, and a whimper escaped her lips. Swallowing hard, she pushed the pain away and tried her best to look serious. She didn't want them to think of her as weak. By the time they laid her down on a stretcher, she was battling with consciousness from the pain, stress, and exhaustion.

The ship they took her to was larger than a space station. The corridors went on forever and were even large and spacious in parts. Passing in and out of consciousness, she saw marble statues on pedestals, large digiscreen windows with scenes of nature or beautiful paintings. All of it was finer than anything she had ever seen in the dome or since.

"Is my brother here?" she asked. There was a proper hospitaller there now in her uniform with the insignia of her order, a white cross and star overlaying the caduceus staff.

The room's lights were blindingly bright. She squinted and looked around for Lady Vardan or any other familiar face.

"Sorry, dear, I don't know." The physician continued poking at her legs and hips.

The pain was nearly unbearable, and she shouted every obscenity she had ever learned in the alleyways of Notus City. "God's bones! It hurts so sarding much."

"We're going to take you for X-rays, but your femur is broken very badly. You may also have fractures in your hip. It's a miracle you're still alive. We'll need to perform surgery to fix the damage. Have you ever had surgery before?"

The woman asked the question like it was the most common thing in the nine worlds. No one like her could afford surgery. Quality medical care was for the wealthy and connected. Everyone outside the high districts had a story of a family member who died because there was nothing the physicians would or could do. That was one of the first lessons she learned living outside the dome.

"No, I can't afford it."

The woman smiled sympathetically. "Don't worry, dear, Grand Marshal Vardan is seeing to your care. You'll get the very best we can offer you."

A team of nurses began to buzz around her, even when she tried to protest. They didn't listen, and she was powerless to stop them. The other major lesson she learned was that no one did anything for free. Whatever Lady Vardan wanted was going to be big. Why else go to so much trouble helping her?

CHAPTER
13

Arabella

January, 4089 U.E.T. – Interlunar Space, Saturn

Weeks went by, and she languished as a prisoner in every way but by name, even if the hospitallers treated her like a queen when it came to her comfort. They avoided any real conversation. Instead of answers, she got empty and long-winded platitudes and prayers for her wellbeing. It wasn't appropriate to question miracles of course. Not that she cared any longer.

Arabella asked about her brother, the missing lifeboats from Buckley's ship, and when Lady Vardan would speak to her again. She received the same answer. "Soon, dear."

Her leg was held together with metal rods that made it so she couldn't move without assistance for weeks. The contraption made her look more machine than human.

It felt almost blasphemous to rely on machinery in her time of need instead of God's grace. At least that was what the cleric back in the dome would have said. Admittedly, she hadn't spent much time worrying about it.

There was a short woman with thinning gray hair who came to see her weekly. She wore bishops' robes, and the regularity of her visit allowed Arabella to keep track of how long she had been aboard the Void Knight's ship.

The longer this strange purgatory went on, she considered they were deciding what crimes they could charge her with then make her healthy enough to stand trial before burning her at the stake in some public square. It was common practice during the Midnight Raids, so it didn't seem impossible.

She busied her mind with anything she could to avoid thinking about Jordan and what had happened to him. She mostly focused on her rehabilitation, so when the time came to move, she would be able to. It had been at least eight weeks in total since her life finally crumpled completely.

The rest of the time, she stared at the digiscreen beside her bed. There wasn't much programming. A few movies and official republic news channels that clicked on occasionally like they always did, whether she wanted them to or not.

Her new favorite was to put on a screensaver showing a tropical beach on Venus. The sun was burning large and bright in the sky and palm trees swayed in the steady breeze. It was so unlike anything she had ever known. Part of her thought it had to be fake. She was so sucked in by the image that she didn't hear the pair of soldiers enter the room.

"Miss, we need you to come with us."

"Is there news about my brother?" she asked hopefully. She never had soldiers visit her. She moved her legs slowly off the bed. She wore a pair of shorts that didn't interfere with the brace on her leg and a baggy sweatshirt that bore the Void Knights logo on it.

One of the soldiers grabbed her crutches and offered to help. "Sorry, miss. I don't know anything about that." He was staring at the metal cage holding her leg together. Metal rods pierced her skin at regular intervals, before passing through the bone and out the other side. "Does it hurt?"

She grimaced as her weight transferred to her feet. Her leg and hip protested mightily. It was a good thing she was always skinny. The physicians wanted her to keep moving as much as possible. She obliged them because the stiffness was infinitely worse if she didn't.

She gave the soldier a sarcastic smile. He wasn't much older than she was. "Nah, it feels sarding great."

No one around her ever knew anything. These soldiers wore regular Republic naval uniforms, so she assumed it was true. They weren't a part of Void Knight business. The soldier got the message and didn't ask any more stupid questions.

The halls of the medical bay were familiar to her, since it was the only place she was allowed to roam freely. It was a welcome treat when they led her out into the main corridors. The ship felt like a small city with people coming and going in every direction.

Some gave her curious looks, but most didn't seem interested at all, either because it was better not to know things or the presence of injured civilians wasn't very noteworthy. Both options seemed less than reassuring.

She admired the marble statues and large paintings as much as she could while trying to keep up. Occasionally she requested to stop for a rest when her hips or leg began to ache too much. The soldiers offered to fetch a wheelchair, but she didn't want that. She could manage this way. The pain was a good reminder that she wasn't safe and free yet.

After they walked what felt like several kilometers, they arrived at a large hub of activity. People came and went through large glass doors bearing the seal of the Void Knights. She assumed this was where they kept their offices aboard the ship.

The doors opened automatically when they approached. Inside, she was handed off to another set of guards. These were older and more serious-looking men than the last. She wagered none of them had ever laughed before.

They led her to a small waiting room that was richly decorated with a plush carpet and banners on the wall. A flag of the Republic was prominently displayed alongside portraits of the Vox and Manus.

Along the wall was a small sofa and chair. In the chair sat a very old-looking man. His face was grizzled, and his bald head was covered in blue geometric tattoos, although his scalp was so splotchy from age that the lines blended. It was the most ornate Jeevan she had ever seen.

He wore faded blue robes with a heavy leather belt around his midsection. On the belt was a large knife. He nodded as she approached. She sat on the sofa as far away from him as possible.

Near the door was a small desk with a young officer in a well-pressed uniform sitting behind it. He was maybe a few years older than her. Blond hair neatly quaffed to the side. He looked at Arabella's leg and smiled sadly, like she was an injured alley dog.

"The Grand Marshal will be available soon," the soldier said in Armanic. His accent was even more unnatural than Arabella's.

"I speak Standard," she said in the finest Inner System accent she could manage.

The man smiled politely and switched to speaking Standard. "My apologies. I shouldn't have assumed."

"No, you shouldn't have." Arabella was tired of people thinking she was a Far Coast peasant who hadn't mastered the intricacies of speech.

The man pursed his lips, obviously unsure of what to say. He was saved by the chime of the phone on the desk. "Yes, Grand Marshal." He stood up and motioned for Arabella to follow. "You can follow me, please."

The office was large and spacious with a separate seating area flanked by a large wooden desk that Lady Vardan was sitting behind. In front of the desk were two chairs. One was occupied by a short-haired man in ornately adorned white robes. Around his neck he wore a gold chain with the star and cross of the Republic. That he was a bishop was clear to her, but why he was there she couldn't say.

Lady Vardan indicated she should take the empty seat. "I'm glad to see you're doing well. I'm sorry I've been too busy to visit sooner."

Arabella bowed to the bishop before sitting as gracefully as she could, placing the crutches on the floor beside the chair. "I understand you must be very busy, but no one will tell me anything. I've been trying to get news about my brother for weeks."

Lady Vardan nodded, her arms folded on the table. "I'm afraid I don't have good news."

Arabella's heart sank, and she saw the image of Jordan bleeding in her arms. "He's dead then too."

"His body was not recovered. All we can say for sure is he wasn't among the life rafts we found."

"But you're still looking," she stated firmly.

"No, I'm afraid not. We have our own mission to accomplish, which brings me to you," she said, shuffling several papers on her desk. Arabella noticed the stack included her identification documents.

"Your mission has something to do with me?" she said sheepishly.

"That will depend on what you have to say. Beside you is Bishop Aschoff. He is here as a liaison of the Council of Bishops."

"Hello, child. I trust you will be forthcoming in your testimony before me and God," he said. His voice was silky and oozed superiority. That he didn't mention Lady Vardan spoke volumes about what he thought of her importance, even if he was forced to defer to her.

"Of course, Bishop. I live to serve," she said, bowing her head as was expected. "But I don't know what I'm supposed to testify to."

"As you know, the Armanic people are a cornerstone of the Republic," Lady Vardan said. "However, since the Midnight Raids, interplanetary crime has been on the rise. Bishop Aschoff is here as part of my effort to identify and apprehend Republic dissidents within Armanic communities of the Far Coast."

"It's important you tell us everything, however unimportant it might seem to you," the bishop said.

Arabella nodded, panic rising in her chest. They must already know everything about the Coalition shipment. Maybe they also knew who she really was... But then again, if they did, why wasn't she already in chains?

Lady Vardan picked up a paper and began reading it. "Your ship was captured by the Lunese pirates outside the orbit of Ymir. Is that accurate?"

Arabella stuck to her story. "It's my parents' ship. The pirates tried to rob us at the way station on Phoebe. The security forces intervened, but some of the pirates persisted in harassing us. My...parents were killed trying to protect us. My brother and I were able to escape."

The bishop looked dubious. "Your brother is younger than you, yes? About eight years old?" Arabella nodded. "The two of you were able to fight off a band of pirates? Also why did you come to Ymir. Didn't you know it's uninhabited?"

Arabella shook her head. She tried to stick as close to the truth as possible. "My father did most of the fighting. He used to be a knight. Him and my mother distracted a pair of pirates while we got away."

Lady Vardan said, "We've retrieved the security footage, although some of it was damaged. It looked like your quick thinking and steady aim saved you and your brother."

"Why wasn't I shown this footage?" the bishop interjected.

"As I said, much of the footage was damaged. It will be shared as part of our final report."

Arabella remained quiet, watching the two verbally spar. It might be a ploy for her to put her guard down.

"Is it true you were unable to unload your cargo at the Phoebe way station due to the attack by the pirates?" Lady Vardan asked next. "I believe you had a shipment of...electrical wire?"

Now Arabella was truly confused. She had never mentioned they were meant to deliver the shipment at Phoebe, but if Ymir was uninhabited it would be reasonable for them to assume that. In any case, it was confirmation they didn't have access to the original contract.

The bishop said, "You didn't answer my previous question. Why were you going to Ymir? What were you expecting to find there?"

Lady Vardan and the bishop looked intently at her, waiting for an answer. "I... Yes, my parents sent me into the way station to find the vendor who was receiving our goods, but I never found him before we were attacked. Once we ran, my only goal was to get away. I knew Ymir was empty. It's why we didn't try and stop. I didn't expect to find anything there at all. I just wanted to get away." She turned to look at Lady Vardan. "I don't know what was in the shipment. I never looked in the crates."

That they didn't mention the Coalition gave her hope they didn't know much at all.

"As you said, your parents were killed in the fighting on Phoebe. Their bodies were identified as Michelle and Alfred Smith. Is that accurate?" Lady Vardan said.

Arabella's heart skipped a beat, and she resisted the urge to smile. They had no idea. "Yes, that's right. My brother's name is Jordan."

The bishop let out an exasperated sigh. "What is your family's association with the vermin? I don't believe you came all this way to deliver some wires."

Arabella shook her head forcefully. He was referring to the Vermilion Coalition. "None at all. A lot of specialty equipment comes from Titan that can't be easily found this far away. These jobs tend to pay the best. It was a long trip, so they took me and my brother with them."

"What else were you transporting that was valuable enough that the pirates would keep chasing you to retrieve?" the bishop said.

That was a question Arabella couldn't easily answer. At least without admitting they were carrying something valuable for the Coalition or the bounty. "I... I don't know. Maybe they wanted the ship."

The bishop scoffed, "You'll have to do better than that. That rust bucket was hardly worth the fuel they burned to catch you."

Arabella had no idea what to say. She was frozen, panic rising, except Lady Vardan bailed her out. "Perhaps the pirates, like you, assumed their cargo was more valuable than it was."

The bishop's lip turned up in the hint of a snarl. "My Lady, your softness for these people continues to be off-putting." He looked over Arabella's injured leg. "Especially to expend such resources on someone unworthy of it."

"We are all God's children, are we not?" Lady Vardan said, sitting back in her chair. "I'll not see any child suffer if it can be avoided."

Arabella wanted to say more to defend herself but decided staying quiet was the safer option. She already seemed to be winning.

"God's light must be earned," he drawled. "Several of the captured pirates mentioned something about waiting to recover a bounty. What do you know about that?"

This at least was a question she had been anticipating. She shrugged. "There are always bounties available in Titan. From the bishop's office, local magistrates, and nearly half a dozen other places."

What she said was true. It was becoming clear to her that this bishop only saw her as another random ice rat. This time, she would use it to her advantage. "We always paid all our bills."

He looked at her like she was an idiot. "No one is chasing a ship through interlunar space to collect a peasant's delinquent debt. Do you even know how much it costs to operate a corvette the size the pirates had?"

She had no idea, so she answered honestly. "I'm sorry, Bishop, I don't. This was my first time traveling so far from home. I've never seen a corvette before up close."

The bishop shook his head and stood abruptly. "I didn't expect you would. My Lady, I will take my leave. Please include anything else you find in your report."

Arabella rose unsteadily on one leg and bowed her head in deference.

Lady Vardan remained seated. When the bishop was out of the room, she motioned for Arabella to sit back down. "I have a few more things to discuss."

"Everything I told the bishop is all I know," she said defensively.

Lady Vardan straightened the stack of papers and then set them aside in a folder. "I believe you."

"I..." She stopped herself.

"You can speak freely, child."

She took a deep breath. "I don't understand why you've helped me so much."

"Like I said, I don't want to see anyone suffer if it can be avoided," Lady Vardan said, her emerald-green eyes piercing deeply into her.

Arabella didn't think that was enough to explain this level of kindness or why she was still in this room. Why would this powerful woman or the bishop give up so much time for her?

"What happens to me now? To my brother?"

"We will continue to operate in the Saturnalian system for a time. We have put out an alert to look for your brother and any missing crew members from the pirates' vessel. That is the best I can offer you. We can't stay here to continue the active search," she said.

Arabella hated the idea of giving up but didn't think there was much else she could do. She had no ship or money to even begin looking. "Thank you," she said weakly. "But then what about me. Am I under arrest?"

"No, the bishop thinks you're involved in some sinister plot, but I think you were in the wrong place at the wrong time. My focus is on capturing the remaining pirates and ensuring justice is done. Is my assessment accurate?" Lady Vardan said, an eyebrow raised.

Arabella swallowed but nodded slowly. She was trying to quickly process everything she knew. Lady Vardan seemed like a smart and shrewd woman. She would need to be to become Grand Marshal of the Void Knights. Surely there was a trap here somewhere, but then there was one glaring detail.

How was it that they were anywhere near Ymir's orbit if it was in fact a dead moon? Arabella considered there could be a secret Republic base, but then why did the Coalition want a delivery sent there? Unless the delivery was meant to be a trap.

She decided to ask, "How did you find the pirate's corvette when you did?"

Lady Vardan crossed her arms. "You were lucky we were in the area on our return from Triton. Our long-range scanners picked up what looked like a larger ship following a smaller one. That it was pirates seemed likely, so it was our duty to investigate."

Arabella pinched her lips. As far as she knew, the explanation seemed plausible, unless the real answer was that they were tracking the Coalition shipment somehow. Maybe it had been a plan to capture her mother and Kasperi all along.

"God must have been watching out for me," she said.

Lady Vardan smiled. "As for what happens next, you have two options. Obviously, you can't remain here." She tapped the table with her finger. "So your first option is we can deliver you back to your home on Titan."

Arabella knew immediately that wasn't an option she wanted. Mizraei would still be there waiting. On the one hand, she welcomed getting her revenge but also knew she wasn't ready. He had far too many resources and friends. "What's the other option?"

"I'm sending a ship to Mercury, but they will make a stop at Luna. There I have a contact who would be able to help you." She handed Arabella a business card.

The card was made of heavy plastic. It was sleek and stylized with a golden logo depicting an atomic model. It read, *Qilin Reinhold, Chief Executive Officer, Kepler Dynamics, Pallas City, Luna.* On the back was some kind of scannable code. "I don't understand."

"The man on that card is a magnate on Luna, a great titan of industry. He has the means to see you're given a chance to succeed in life, more than you will have if you remain on Titan."

Arabella stared at the woman. If it was true, what she was offering was beyond any sense of honor or nobility. Arabella was nobody. She latched on to the only explanation. "Are you doing this because you feel guilty for getting my brother killed?"

The woman returned her stare, and Arabella felt her confidence wither. This wasn't a woman she could intimidate or cajole. "It's bold of you to question me like this. You would throw aside my goodwill by insulting me to my face?"

Arabella averted her eyes and stared at the dark veins clearly visible under her alabaster skin. The blue lines reminded her of the unrelenting ice. In the ice, she found her resolve and looked back at Lady Vardan.

"I have nothing left to lose. Everyone who meant something to me is dead. I don't mean to insult you, Lady Vardan."

"Do you want to throw away your life?"

"No," Arabella said firmly. If she did, she would go back to Titan and confront Mizraei for what he had done. "I'm only trying to understand. I'm no one, but you're offering me this opportunity. The army is full of thousands of Armanic kids like me."

Lady Vardan leaned forward, interlocking her fingers on the desk. "Maybe, but not all of them have fought off a ship's worth of pirates while trying to save their brother." Arabella was about to disagree, but Lady Vardan raised a finger and picked up the phone. "Lieutenant, can you send in Mr. Maharaj please? I think this might provide more perspective for you."

The old man from the waiting room entered a moment later. He approached the desk and offered Lady Vardan a courtly bow, before settling into the empty chair beside Arabella.

"My Lady, thank you for allowing me to be here," he said.

"Of course, Mr. Maharaj. It's my pleasure after the help you've given me through the campaign," Lady Vardan said, and Arabella thought she meant it.

"His holiness seemed unhappy when he left. I take it his quest for dissidents continues," the man said with a toothy grin. He turned to Arabella. "Lady Vardan told me of your exploits. Quite impressive."

Arabella scrunched her brow. "I'm sorry, sir, but who are you?"

"I am Ashoka Maharaj, Khatak and advisor to the Duke of Triton. When I heard of your story, I asked Lady Vardan if I could meet you personally."

"It's true. He insisted many times, but the bishop wanted to be sure you weren't a terrorist first," Lady Vardan said.

"A Khatak... It's an honor, sir," Arabella said, feeling embarrassed. The Khataks were Armanic Chroniclers, something between a priest and a librarian. They were the ones who decided who did or didn't receive a Jeevan. "I've never met one before. Never even seen one actually."

The man nodded solemnly. "We are rarer than I wish, but we try to maintain the old traditions. It's why I wanted to see you. I heard your tale, and it's worthy of a Jeevan." He motioned to the one painted on his head. "A Jeevan is made of many saans, or lines, and I'm here to provide your first. The start of your story."

Arabella didn't know what to say. "I... No..."

Lady Vardan said, "When I first saw you, I said you were a testament to your people. I have known a great many Armanics. It wasn't an empty compliment."

Arabella didn't know what to say. She felt like a fraud. She had denied her Armanic heritage so many times, lied and concealed, leading to the events that got her family killed. The events they were now celebrating her for.

"I don't deserve that honor. I'm only fourteen. I... I only got lucky."

The man placed a hand on her shoulder and leaned in close. "It's your choice whether you wear the mark. You can wear it on your face or close to your heart. That choice is also yours, whether or not you deserve it. Well, that is my choice to make. I've heard your story and judged it worthy."

She wanted to shout that it was all a lie but couldn't find the courage. The Jeevan was all she ever wanted since she was a little girl. Seeing it on Kasperi's face, knowing what it meant to her people and history. It was an honor beyond anything the Republic's clergy could give her.

"When do I have to decide?"

Ashoka reached under his heavy robes and pulled out a small bundle. "I would prefer you decide now. If Lady Vardan is willing, she can serve as the witness."

The woman smiled broadly, her stoney expression cracking for the first time. "It's been a long time since I've been a witness. If Arabella agrees, I would be honored. What do you say, child?"

Ashoka rolled out his bundle revealing a tattoo gun and a collection of inks.

Arabella swallowed hard, brushing strands of hair away from her face. If she didn't take this offer, would she ever get another one? Could she live with the shame of knowing it was all a lie? She didn't have enough time to figure it all out. Ultimately her heart wanted a way to connect with her past and build a new future.

"I will wear it on my face," she said, like Kasperi had. "Do I get to choose what it will look like?"

Ashoka thought for a moment. "You will receive the saans which is a single line. Normally, I receive the answer from God on how it should be applied, but maybe God has given you the answer instead. Speak and I will listen."

She considered what he said but didn't think God had anything to do with it. "I would like it to split my face," she traced a finger from the corner of her hairline down to the opposite corner of her jaw.

Lady Vardan tilted her chin, perhaps trying to understand the meaning. Arabella wasn't going to explain it but thankfully neither asked.

Ashoka nodded. "Very well. I warn you this will hurt," he looked down to her leg. "But I wager you're up for it."

She nodded and sank back into the chair as much as she could. The line would represent how she was divided between two worlds, each half distinctly shaped by the story of her life.

"Tell me, where were you born?"

She considered lying. "Does it matter?"

He motioned to the array of the inks in his bundle. Some were blue, while others were shades of gray, brown, and even red. "Each ink is made from the soil or ice of different worlds. The first saans should come from the land of your birth. The rest will come from where you earn your next saans."

That they weren't all shades of blue surprised her. She had never seen a Jeevan that wasn't blue. Arabella considered all her lies. She had told everyone she was from Titan, but never that she was born there. "Enceladus," she said finally.

He reached for one of the blue inks. She watched him test the machine almost in a ritualistic fashion. His fingers glided in delicate motions over the knobs and settings. The ink reservoir was filled with slow reverent drops, and he dipped the tip of the needle into it like a priest blessing water. Lady Vardan rose to stand beside him, her arms crossed at her back.

The room no longer felt like an office aboard a starship. Something about the ritual was comforting. Her apprehension began to melt away, and she felt a deeper connection than she should have. She was in a strange place with people she didn't know, yet she felt connected to them.

Arabella said, "Were you a cleric before you became a Khatak?"

Ashoka shook his head. "No, I am a warrior like you. Why do you ask."

Like her... She wasn't a warrior, at least not yet, but she would certainly try to live up to the name. "Something about what you're doing reminds me of rituals the clerics do."

He nodded as if he understood. "Not all sanctuaries look like churches when you're far from home."

"What?"

"An old saying," Ashoka said. "Are you ready?"

She nodded. Had she been looking for a sanctuary? The needle bit into her skin, and she flinched, her eye twitching involuntarily.

"Do you want a leather strap to bite down on?" Lady Vardan asked. Her tone wasn't condescending. That she didn't move to offer a hand to hold or any other physical comfort was also telling. This was a woman who valued inner strength.

"No, I can manage," she said, clenching her jaw. The pain was sharp and fiery. Her skin itched and burned in equal measure, and it felt like the needle was piercing her skull. She welcomed the pain. She deserved so much more for the lies she had told.

She tried to breathe and think of that sense of sanctuary she had only a moment earlier. Her mind took her back to the dome. Jordan was playing with a toy truck, while mother watched, a gleam in her eye. Kasperi stood nearby speaking with Father in hushed whispers. Everything seemed happy and normal. Her calm vanished when she remembered it was all a happy lie.

Her lips quivered, and tears ran down her face. They mixed with the ink and became part of her story.

One day, an opportunity would come to make things right. She would be ready to grasp it and turn this mark of shame into something honorable. If not, she could die as the same coward she was now.

CHAPTER
14

The preceding months leading up to her arrival in Lunese orbit had been long and depressing. After agreeing to depart for Luna, she was quickly transferred to her new ship, a wholly unremarkable Republic Naval frigate. It was far smaller and much less interesting than the monstrous ship she had been residing on.

Her leg had healed enough that the steel rods were removed, and she was able to return to regular activities. She spent time in the ship's gym and tried to regain her lost strength. Since she had no official role aboard the vessel, she had too much free time to sit and wallow in her feelings of loneliness.

She fought herself about the choice to go to Luna. Ultimately, she knew it was the right one under the circumstances. There was no chance of a life for her on Titan any longer. But it had been her home for a long time.

The choice that bothered her more was the one to receive the Jeevan. She didn't recognize herself any longer when she looked in the mirror, and the sight of the heavy blue line only left her disgusted. She didn't deserve it, no matter what Ashoka had said. He based his opinion on lies she had allowed to continue.

The crew of the ship barely paid attention to her. She had tried to be friendly in the beginning, excited to be a part of a new community. But when she talked to younger members of the crew, she would get short, stunted answers that left no room for further conversation. They were dismissive, even if they weren't rude. Arabella got the impression they were told not to interact with her. She wasn't one of them.

136

That left her with the other non-military personnel, clergy and Void Knight clerks who were more than twice her age. The majority had no interest in speaking with her, and the ones who did were more interested in exploiting the relationship they perceived she had with Lady Vardan. None of their social maneuvering interested her in the slightest. Her fifteenth birthday came and went in March, and she spent it alone.

Lady Vardan wasn't her friend. A benefactor maybe, but not much else. She had no illusions she would ever hear from the woman again, now that her conscience had been settled over her inability to find Jordan. The more time Arabella had with her thoughts, the more she became convinced that was the only reason Lady Vardan helped her, to assuage her guilt.

The captain announced when they entered Lunese orbit, but after months of malaise, Arabella's heart didn't flutter, and she felt no sense of wonder. Luna was another place now, devoid of hope and family.

In a quiet corner of the ship was a hangar bay with a large glass viewport. She went there now, like she had the last several days. It was still "nighttime" for the ship, and the hangar bay was mostly empty like she expected. There were a couple of mechanics working on one of the Falcons. They looked up when she entered, but seeing who it was, they waved absently and continued their work. They couldn't even say hello.

Arabella continued into a narrow corridor in the corner of the hangar bay. In the dark cavity was a small airlock intended for workers exiting the ship to conduct repairs. She raised a keycard she had stolen from one of the mechanics days earlier and pressed it to the controls. The first door slid open quietly on well-greased rollers without raising any alarms. She passed through the first threshold.

Inside, she was bathed in the feint glow of red lights that were designed to keep people away. Along with written messages highlighting the many hazards. "Turn back now, you idiot. It isn't safe here," they boldly said. She ignored the warnings and stepped deeper, stopping at the large door, the only thing separating her from the infinite void.

The door had a large window she had looked out several times before. Now she used it to see Luna for the first time. The lunar surface was a sea of lights on a scale she'd never seen before. Unlike Titan, there was no thick atmosphere to hide the surface.

The cloud cover was sparse, and where the sun shone, she could see endless gray deserts interspersed with deep and shadowy craters. The gray was only broken by the reflection of lakes and dark seas that threatened to swallow her.

She looked for any sign of life beyond the glow of lights. There were domed areas with their vibrant green treasures locked away inside. Those areas were restricted, and she had no claim to their riches, so she kept her eyes moving. The endless gray deserts offered no sign of a lush world she could see from this vantage. There were also no great ice sheets to make her feel welcome.

After so much time spent aboard starships, all she wanted was grass she could run her fingers through. Or a patch of snow to lie down in and feel the warmth of the sun and the chill on her back. She expected Luna to be at least a whisper of old Earth and the Garden of Eden, a bright world full of nature and the promise of peace.

She'd only ever found that peace once in her life on the ice of Enceladus. The cold air on her cheeks and ice forming on her eyelashes. The crunch of fresh snow under her boots. The wonder of the geysers shooting into space with Saturn and its rings so close she could reach up and grab them. None of that majesty was here.

Her eyes moved past Luna and settled on Earth. The planet was large, much bigger than any rocky world she had ever seen. It was covered in a mass of roiling clouds and streaking lightning so thick she couldn't see the surface. It was perhaps the only place lonelier than space. A dead world, soiled forever by the mistakes of man.

She wanted so badly to come here once, dreamed of it as a girl and begged her father to take her. Now that she made it, she couldn't see the point. It was all dead, like her family. At least on the ice, water and pressure bubbled under the surface, promising a beautiful and explosive future when it finally broke free.

Precious minerals would rain down, and humans could reap the fruits of God's creation. Here, there was nothing to dream of, nothing promising to make the world better.

Arabella reached into her pocket. She took out the business card Lady Vardan had given her, reading it over. Was this vague promise worth even more pain? She didn't think so. She looked at the airlock controls beside her. It would be easy to start the sequence. There wasn't anyone nearby to stop her.

The door would close behind her, and the window would open, releasing her into the abyss. At least then the cold could claim her for good. Maybe that was the closest she could expect to get to the ice again. In the Celestial City, she could reunite with her family and beg for their forgiveness.

Silent tears rolled down her face as she flipped the first switch to unlock the control panel. Then she held her palm over the button that would activate the airlock opening cycle. She hesitated.

Stop being a coward. Press the button and end it all.

All the pain, all the guilt, all the loneliness.

She was so tired of being alone.

The very thought of stepping on Luna left her with a deeper dread than the empty abyss. At least death would be quick, and someone would be waiting for her. She could make things right and find peace. No one she loved was waiting for her on Luna.

A tear ran down her cheek, and she took a deep breath.

It's time.

Her arm relaxed, and she felt ready, but then there were footsteps behind her.

Arabella's body jerked involuntarily, and she nearly pressed the button anyway. "Who, who's there? I... I was just looking out the window." Why she tried to lie and apologize, she didn't know. She didn't owe whoever this was an explanation. She had to finish what she was doing.

"I am Namtar," he said in a thick accent she didn't recognize, but coupled with his tan skin and dark features, she assumed he was Mercurian. He looked youthful but wore the uniform of a Void Knight. She assumed he must be much older than her. "Please, continue to look." He motioned to the window.

Arabella hadn't seen him on the ship before and was annoyed to see him now. "Can you find another window? I'd prefer to be alone." She didn't try and hide her tears.

"I will stand as a witness to your end."

"What are you talking about?" she said angrily.

"You were going to press that button but hesitated. You fight, you fall, your tale is told. How will anyone tell your tale if no one is here to see how it ends?" he said casually.

She turned to face him, her hand moving off the button. "Are you mocking me? Who the sarding hell are you?"

How could he speak so plainly about her death? Better yet, why did it bother her so much that he did. If she wanted to die, what did it matter what this nobody had to say about it?

"I already said that my name is Namtar, your witness." He moved his arms behind his back. He was shorter than she was but built powerfully. "Every warrior seeks their end eventually. I've known many. I'm not here to mock you."

"I..." She didn't even know what to say. He had unsettled her and distracted her from the despair she felt a moment before. Maybe that was his plan all along. She looked again at his uniform. "Are you with Lady Vardan? Did she send you to keep an eye on me? That's why you showed up here now, isn't it?"

He shook his head, and said with no sign of mirth, "I came to pray and saw you here. That I serve Lady Vardan is unimportant."

"You don't need to try and stop me. I've already made up my mind." She kept her voice low, hoping no one else would come and interrupt them.

"Every warrior makes a choice about when to fight. It's not my choice to make," he said, indicating he hadn't crossed the threshold into the airlock.

"It's only because you don't want me to take you with me." She turned away from him. Arabella was ashamed that he saw the Jeevan and thought she was something she wasn't. "I'm no warrior, only a coward. It's why I'm still here."

"It takes more courage to live than to lie down in the mud. Dying is easy. Cowards die every day."

She laughed, shaking her head. "Such a brave knight to never know fear or lack courage. You probably have a large, wealthy family and your own high position to keep you warm at night." Striding toward him, she jabbed a finger into his chest. "I have an ache in my leg that never goes away and the honor of knowing I'm the last in my bloodline, alone except for my horrid conscious that refuses to stop screaming in my skull."

Namtar smiled warmly and placed a hand on her shoulder. She expected a shallow attempt at comfort, but instead he pushed her past the threshold and deeper into the airlock.

He spoke in a low and firm whisper, "Only cowards and lunatics pretend they lack fear. Fate is inescapable. Go and push the button if it's your destiny to die, then it's also mine. We can exit this plane as warriors together, laughing in the face of our creators."

Arabella stepped back, unable to resist his push. She saw the button was within arm's reach again. "You must be a lunatic then," she said harshly.

"No, we all have a path to walk. You're at a crossroads in yours, and it's time to choose."

"I don't want to kill you. Leave. This has nothing to do with you." Her hand was shaking, and her resolve was all but gone.

"So you will fight your fears to keep me alive?" he said, holding her gaze with his piercing brown eyes.

"I…" He had caught her in a trap. She either killed him or let go of her plan. "I don't know what to do anymore."

"Come and tell me your story, and I will tell you one of mine. That way we can keep each other alive, long after we fall." He held out a hand to her.

She hesitated. It was the kindest gesture she had received since old man Chen taught her to play Go. Reluctantly, she took it and let him lead her out of the airlock, "Thank you."

"Thank fate for bringing us together," he said.

She leaned into him, and to her surprise he easily supported her weight. He was much stronger than his size suggested. It might be temporary, but she appreciated the closeness, even from a stranger.

"What do I do now?" she said, wiping the tears from her eyes.

"A great question to be able to ask yourself. Do you like tea?"

She nodded, and he led her back into the ship, into the light and away from the darkness of the hangar bay and space beyond.

They returned to the ship's mess hall. People were beginning to prepare for the shift change, and the hall was filled with people coming and going.

Arabella took a seat at a far table in the quietest corner. Namtar returned a few minutes later with two cups of hot tea.

She took a deep breath of the hot steam. It was filled with an earthy, floral smell. "This tea smells wonderful. It isn't something they normally serve."

"No, but you're with me now," he said, smiling.

She looked at him seriously. "Why did you help me, really?"

"I've struggled like you before, but I had teachers to help me through it."

"I have nothing to offer you in return."

"Give your life purpose, and I will be happy. Lady Vardan saw potential in you, and that is a great honor," he said, picking up the cup of hot tea. He took a deep swig.

She picked up her own cup to sip. She pulled back when the hot liquid burned her tongue. "God's bones, that's hot. I thought you said you weren't here because of Lady Vardan."

He shrugged. "That isn't what I said. She didn't ask me to do any of this. I'm here for another purpose, but if I can accomplish my goals while helping you, I will. As I said, fate brought us together."

He sounded like a madman or some false prophet. She wanted to reject his offer, but she had no good reason to besides her own stubbornness. Following her instincts had gotten her into this mess. Maybe it was time to try and do things differently.

"You said you would tell me a story."

He nodded slowly. "I'm also the last of my line, like you. My family died while I stood powerless to do anything. I watched as they were killed, one by one, before I found the courage to pick up my spear."

"Was it pirates?" she asked, her heart breaking at the thought of it.

"No, a neighbor who thought what was ours should be his. They came in the night when everyone was asleep," he said, taking another swig of the tea.

"How old were you?"

"I was twelve. I had only just earned my spear."

"Was this back on Mercury?" she asked, amazed by the details. She didn't know they had such a warrior culture. What did he mean by earning his spear? He had been even younger than she was. "Did you get your revenge?"

"Eventually, when I raised my spear against my enemies, yes. I lost my family but found the warrior's path. Ever since, I've tried to honor them through my actions. In return, they watch over me and give me strength," he said, ignoring the first part of her question. "Now tell me your story."

She swallowed hard before beginning. At first, the story trickled out like a leaky faucet. Then the pressure became lighter as she spoke, and eventually she opened the flood gates.

She left out potentially incriminating details but otherwise told him everything, all that had happened since her dad was attacked on the ice. Namtar listened intently, his eyes never wavering. When she was done, her tears had dried, and she felt like a stone had been lifted from her chest.

He put a rough hand over hers on the table. "I will hold your tale in confidence. You've shown great courage to make it this far."

"I'm not sure I can make it much further." She handed him the business card. "I'm supposed to go see this man. Do you know him?"

Namtar looked over the card and nodded. "He is a good man. That Lady Vardan sent you to him is telling. She hasn't sent many prospects to Qilin."

She scrunched her brow. "Do you know what this is all about?"

"Yes, although I can't say very much. He is a great magnate involved in many industries. As part of his philanthropy, he takes a great interest in sponsoring talent for the trials."

Her eyes widened. "You mean for entry to the Special Warfare Academies, like to join the Pandora Fleet or Republican Guard?"

"The Frumentarii also recruit from the SWAs, but yes."

She had thought this might have been about a low-level office job or maybe some kind of security duty. Instead, Namtar was suggesting it could be a path to a real career with a real future, the life she dreamed of back in the dome and told Kasperi she wanted. The kind of future that could give her the means to return to Titan one day and face Mizraei again. "What will I have to do?"

"You will compete at a series of challenges, and the best candidates will be given the best opportunities, like admission to the leadership academies, where you would train to become an officer. The worst may be sent away entirely."

She felt a new sense of dread rising in her throat. "What if I don't qualify? I have nowhere to go."

Namtar smiled broadly. "I will make sure you're ready."

CHAPTER
15

Finding Namtar that night in the hangar was a new turning point in her life. She was still horribly scared when she set foot on the Lunar surface, but at least she wasn't alone. He claimed Lady Vardan hadn't sent him to keep an eye on her, and she chose to believe him, even if it seemed unlikely. Maybe all she needed was an excuse to keep going, however flimsy.

Arabella learned very little about him beyond the obvious. He was a Knight Captain serving within the fighting branch of the Knights of the Void. This was also when she learned the nine knightly orders all had a martial branch beyond their normal lawyers and bureaucrats. He was on some mission he couldn't discuss, but as much as he was able, he would see to her wellbeing until she left for her eventual training. So he became her escort.

From the ship, they had private transport for the two of them. Namtar took her to a high-district hotel located in one of the many monstrous spires in the city center that clustered like a sleeping porcupine on the gray plains of Luna. The buildings were thin and numerous, clad in steel and glass that shone brightly in the morning sun. The low gravity and obvious wealth of the moon made it easy for them to reach for the heavens.

She hadn't realized it from orbit, but the Sun was everything she ever dreamed it would be from the surface. Even if it didn't dominate the sky like Saturn had back home. It shone infinitely brighter. On the landing pad of the hotel she stood, her eyes closed, head turned to the bright bulb. The heat washed over her skin, and she shivered from the excitement of it. Warmth. Real warmth.

"Why isn't everyone out here enjoying this?" she said.

"Not everyone appreciates how precious a new dawn is," Namtar said. He didn't try to rush her along.

She took a deep breath and turned away. Her eyes squinting hard against the blinding light. "I think I might need sunglasses. I guess this must be nothing for you compared to Mercury."

He laughed. "It's all the same dawn." He motioned for her to follow him toward the entrance of the spire. "Your eyes will adjust, but sunglasses are a good idea."

"I think I could stay standing out there until they do."

"You'll have time, and you should take it to enjoy this moment. I wish I could experience these wonders again for the first time. There's no greater blessing," he said and left her to wait in the marble clad lobby while he went to the reception desk.

She admired the building's interior, gawking at the expanse of natural materials and a distinct lack of plastic. Paintings hung on the walls, and plush sofas wrapped in leather sat on equally plush carpets. She could see the surfaces were worn and damaged in places, but everything shone brightly. It was old but not neglected.

She was becoming slightly desensitized to the grandeur she continued to experience. From Lady Vardan's starship to this beautiful hotel. Then there was the multitude of people living on Luna that was hard for her brain to comprehend.

While cities on Titan were relatively small and compact, here they were sprawling and massive. The notion that it was a den of pirates went out of her head immediately as some unfortunate rumor. The gleam of polished marble and glass didn't match what she knew of pirates.

Namtar returned, handing her a key to her own room. His would be beside hers. It was the first time she had ever had a room to herself. "I need to attend to some business. If you need me, call. I'll have my comm device close by."

Arabella hesitated at the idea of him leaving but knew he had work to do, so his leaving didn't come as a total surprise. "I'm going to go and visit Kepler Industries."

She was anxious to find out who Lady Vardan was sending her to and what it would mean for her future.

Namtar nodded and handed her several more credit chips. "So you don't have to spend your own." He motioned for the concierge to approach them. "Can you arrange transportation for Miss Smith?"

"Yes, sir, right away."

Arabella felt uncomfortable with the formality. She would have to try and remember her mother's old etiquette lessons. Miss Smith. She had forgotten how to be Lady Serra and got used to being Arabella. Miss Smith, however, would be someone new.

She didn't have any luggage besides a small backpack, so she didn't need to go to her room first. She could explore it later.

The journey was quick, and the transport ship dropped her off at a high-altitude landing platform. It was far removed from the ground level, and she wondered what was down there in the shadowy depths. The buildings were so densely packed and tall that they left many shadowy areas. It was so dark in spots that bright neon lights were visible even in the daylight.

The landing port was busy with various ships coming and going. Giving the illusion the building was inhaling and exhaling humanity. There was only one direction to go, and she walked the short distance to the large steel arched doorways. The pillars were arranged in a dazzling architectural layout that resembled the prow of an old seafaring vessel.

There were armored security personnel at the door, men and women wearing ballistic vests and carrying large rifles. They eyed each passing person. She worried she might be stopped, but they only briefly glanced her way.

Most of the people in the lobby wore business attire. Men and women alike, dressed in stylish suits with perfectly quaffed hair. There was a small minority with smooth skin that hadn't been ravaged by radiation. They were the high-district natives.

Most of the others dressed in a similar fashion, but their skin showed subtle signs of the hardships of growing up in the mid and lower districts. Their clothing was also slightly less fine.

The people were diverse with dark-skinned Mercurians and blond-haired Venusians interspersed with pale-skinned Jovians or Armanics and everything in between. There were even obviously low-district workers in janitorial uniforms who shuffled around with brooms in their hands, avoiding eye contact with the others. Their stooped backs and short statures made them easy to spot.

Admiring all the fashionable clothing left her feeling very self-conscious. She was still wearing borrowed exercise clothes with the Void Knight insignia on it, long pants and a baggy sweater that left her looking sloppy. Her long silvery brown hair was barely contained in a bun. She hoped the knightly insignias kept her from being confused with a vagrant. Maybe she should have primped herself at the hotel before she came, but at least so far no one had tried to stop her.

The lobby was a massively vaulted room that echoed dramatically. The heels of hard-leather shoes clacked loudly on marble tiles among the soft hum of voices. In the rear were turnstiles that led to large lift pods that shot ever upward into the core of the structure.

Unsure of what else to do, she approached the reception desk, which was manned by no fewer than six people. She waited patiently for one of them to call her over. A kind-looking man with a straight back and a welcoming smile called out, "Hello, miss, how may we help you today?"

"I'm not sure, but I was given this." She handed him the plastic business card Lady Vardan had given her.

The man's expression never changed as he took the card, stashing it quickly behind the desk. "Thank you. Can I have your name please?"

"Arabella Smith," she said. "So what do I do now? Can I get the card back?" She felt uncomfortable that he had taken it without any explanation.

"You won't need it any longer." He typed several things into a digipad before placing it down in front of her. "I'm going to need you to sign here and here," he said, indicating the proper lines.

"What's all this?"

"Standard nondisclosure agreement. Until you sign it, I won't be able to provide you with any additional information." His smile never broke. It was becoming unsettling.

She stared at the document, trying to read the small print carefully.

"I can provide a copy in Armanic, if you prefer."

Her jaw tightened. *Well, that didn't take long*, she thought. "This is fine, thank you."

"We also have other dialects and audio versions..."

"*This is fine.*"

The man nodded. "No problem. We only try to be accommodating."

She finished reading, and nothing odd stood out to her, besides the fact that Keplar Industries would claim ownership of everything short of her soul, should she divulge any information. Since she had little else but that, the risk seemed manageable. She scribbled her mark and then placed her palm on the screen to sign it.

"Thank you, miss. You can follow me this way," the receptionist said, stepping around the counter to meet her.

He led her to one of the lifts and motioned her inside. She stepped in tentatively. This was another first for her.

The man pressed several buttons, scanned his keycard, and said, "Someone else will meet you for processing. Good luck."

The glass doors shut, and the lift shot to life, launching her into the sky. It caught her off guard, and she reached out for the hand railings. "Sarding hell." Her heart raced, and memories of her sudden deceleration over Ymir raced through her mind.

Thankfully this wasn't that dramatic, but it left her sweaty and frightened. The lift stopped at some impossibly high floor. Her knuckles were locked on the railing, and she was breathing like she had run for miles. When the door opened, she shot out as if the floor would fall out from under her.

A pair of rough-looking men in fine suits were there to greet her. They had guns on their hips but didn't look like Republic military. She assumed they must be private security. They led her through a series of busy offices with rows of cubicles before entering a collection of ornate adjoining rooms. The rooms were even finer than Lady Vardan's had been aboard her ship.

They stopped in a waiting room adjacent to a pair of heavy looking copper doors with a complex design. The markings reminded her vaguely of a Jeevan pattern.

A lithe woman in a pencil skirt with golden-blonde curls draped over her shoulders sat at a large metallic and glass desk beside the door. She stood gracefully to meet Arabella, a digipad in her hand.

"Welcome, Miss Smith. Mr. Reinhold is a busy man, so we'll have to keep this meeting quick." She scanned Arabella's clothing with a look of obvious disappointment. "You will make your case, and if he wishes to proceed with your sponsorship, we will continue with your initial screening. Do you understand?"

The security guards took her backpack and began patting her down, presumably for weapons. "Is this an interview?"

The woman raised an eyebrow. "Of course it is, Miss Smith. What did you think you were doing here?"

Arabella had no idea anymore. The guards gave an all clear, and she wrapped her arms around herself. If this was the type of woman Reinhold hired, what chance would she have looking like a homeless street urchin. She tried to smooth her hair.

"There's no fixing that rats nest now," the assistant said with a sniff. "At least you're clean enough. Something got you this far. Trust that."

This sarding bitch...

Arabella considered hitting the woman before saying, "Understood." If she knew what to expect, she might have taken time to prepare herself. How was she supposed to know? Namtar might not have known either, but it would have been nice if Lady Vardan had taken the time to offer more details. Why did everything have to be so cryptic?

The assistant held a finger up to an earpiece, listening to someone and said, "This way please." She pushed open the door and motioned Arabella inside. It opened easily despite its massive size.

The room was expansive, much more so than the antechamber would have suggested. Glass walls reached up and out like the petals of a flower, giving a nearly unobstructed view of the city's lights and surrounding towers, few of which rivaled this one. Immediately outside the window was what looked like a private landing pad with a sleek and beautiful starship docked on it.

She must have been gawking because the assistant gave her a light push into the room, before exiting and closing the door behind her. Arabella stepped slowly toward the center of the room where there was a large copper desk that matched the doors. Two comfortable-looking chairs were empty in front of it.

Flanking her on either side of the room were a vast number of display cases with all manner of strange and beautiful objects. She wished she could have run over to look at them, but behind the desk was a man waiting for her.

He was slim but not in a gaunt way. He had small wrinkles at the corners of his eyes, and she assumed he was probably in his forties. His short hair was dark-brown and neatly gelled. He wore horn-rimmed glasses and a fashionable navy-blue suit. A gold chain held his necktie in place. It had to be Qilin Reinhold, the CEO of Keplar Industries.

Arabella stopped finally in front of the desk, and said awkwardly, "Uh, hi."

You idiot. Is that really the best you can come up with? she reprimanded herself. She could feel her cheeks flushing and her palms getting sweaty.

Qilin seemed amused. "Hello. Please, have a seat. I'm Qilin Reinhold."

Arabella took one of the empty chairs. It was soft and comfortable, the leather creaking slightly under her weight. "You aren't Lunese?" She had seen enough broadcasts from the capital to recognize a Martian accent. "Um, I'm Arabella Smith," she added quickly.

"Very observant, Miss Smith. No, I'm not, but neither are you."

She braced herself to be called an ice rat, but he only waited for her reply. She said, "I'm from the Far Coast, the Saturnalian system."

He nodded. "I assumed so by the Jeevan. I would have known about someone as young as you earning one here on Luna. Tell me, how is it you came to have one of my coded business cards?"

She hesitated, unsure of what to say. She came here thinking someone else would know why. Then she thought of telling a lie. What if all of this had been some elaborate trap? No, that would be silly. "Lady Vardan gave it to me."

He stared at her, pulling a jeweled cigarette case from his pocket. Lighting a cigarette he said, "Do you know why you're here, Miss Smith?"

"You can call me Arabella." She had grown used to that name even if she hadn't fully owned it yet. "No, Lady Vardan only said you would be able to help me."

He let out a puff of smoke. "Maybe, but this isn't charity. I help those who can help me and more importantly help themselves. Even Lady Vardan's recommendation is not enough to bypass the effort required."

"I'm not looking for handouts. I've never been afraid of hard work." She thought of her father's lesson. "The future is only ours if we're strong enough to hold it."

He quirked his lip. "Where did you hear that?"

"My father, sir."

"He must have been a wise man."

Arabella wasn't so sure, but the man who said it before him probably was. Her father was maybe the only person she knew who had made more mistakes than her. She smiled politely.

Qilin continued, "By the Jeevan on your face, I assume you know the opportunity I'm offering is martial in nature."

"Yes, sir, you're looking for candidates to sponsor for the trials, but I'm not sure I understand why."

"The Republic's premiere military posts, the Frumentarii, Republican Guard, and Pandora Fleet only recruit from the special warfare academies. Furthermore, officers of any military branch must attend one of the military leadership academies. To enter any of these schools, you must pass the trials first. There's no other way to join. It makes the process especially competitive."

"It has always been my dream to serve, sir, but I don't understand why I need a sponsor," she said, adding quickly, "but I'm very happy to have one."

He stared deeply into her eyes, as if weighing something. "Positions in these units come with high salaries and tremendous prestige. Particularly if you make it to a leadership track. There are millions of applicants but only a handful of military academies in the solar system."

She understood that much already so waited till he continued.

"To be considered by an academy, you need to first pass the trials. To enter a trial, there is a significant fee, far outside the reach of most citizens. There are some spots reserved by random lottery, but those are very few."

She wrinkled her nose. That part wasn't familiar, but it made sense. "Why would you pay that expense for a stranger? You said yourself you don't do charity."

Qilin leaned back, crossing his legs. He seemed pleased. "The heart of the issue. Everything is business. If you forget everything else, remember that much. This is a mutually beneficial arrangement. You receive a chance at a good career, and I receive a connection to someone potentially useful."

"I would be indebted to you." She wasn't sure she liked where this was going. She had no interest in servitude, no matter the benefits. It was a situation far too common for people in the Far Coast.

He grabbed a crystal ash tray and knocked off the spent embers from his cigarette, it was nearly half finished. "Not in a literal sense, unless of course you fail to pass the trials. If that happens at fault of your own, you'll be required to return my expenses plus interest. To do that, you would receive an employment contract here at Keplar Industries."

So indentured servitude *was* what he was after. "And if I do pass the trials? Then what."

"You do your duty to the Republic."

"That's it? What's in it for you then?" she asked, even more suspicious.

He shrugged. "A day might come when I call on you for something. I would expect you to answer, whenever or however that might manifest itself."

She hated that he was being so cagey. "Something illegal? None of this is worth it if it ends with me burning at the stake."

"You spoke of the future before, about how it's ours if we're strong enough to grab it. On that we agree. Mankind deserves the best future it can build for itself. Everything I do is toward that end. You could call it my...eternal dream." His face lit up, his mind drifting elsewhere.

Arabella thought he seemed like another rich do-gooder who had no idea what the working-class districts were like. Her quality of life had been quite high for the far end of the solar system. But it probably wasn't much better than a Lunese low or mid district. Still, she never realized how good she had it until she moved to Titan. It was probably the same or worse for people like Reinhold, who grew up with golden spoons.

"You're some kind of reformist?" she said as delicately as such a statement could be said in uncertain company. Being a reformer or a dissident was a thin line in the eyes of the Republic.

Reinhold took one final drag of his cigarette and placed it in the ash tray. "All you need to decide is whether you also want a better future, a future that benefits mankind above all else. I'm afraid our time is up, and you'll need to choose."

She looked at the smoke curling up from the cigarette in the ash tray. It wafted up before turning down sharply toward an air vent on the floor. He seemed to have thought of everything.

She wrung her hands, trying to buy herself time to answer. If she could get a position with the Frumentarii or any of the premier units, it could give her the proper access to find out information on Buckley or Mizraei. She might even be able to leverage her new position to get rid of them for good.

Then again, she could end up a pawn to this magnate's fantasy. Namtar seemed to think this was a good idea, and Lady Vardan trusted this man. That would have to be enough, at least for now. In time, maybe she could break away and use her own money and skills to make a different future. One she chose for herself.

"A better future is all I've ever wanted. If you can give me that, then we're on the same page."

"Excellent." His smile was broad and cheerful, which made her think it might be entirely fake. Magnates were known for being devious after all. "My assistant will see to the next steps. I wish you the best of luck, Miss Smith," he said with a nod, turning his attention back to the digiscreen on his desk.

The assistant returned a moment later to escort her from the room. She was taken to another office on a lower floor where she signed a book's worth of agreements and disclosures. It was more paper than she had ever held at one time.

Then she was taken to a clinical-looking office, still in the same sky-scraper, where a pair of clerks grilled her with questions about her past and upbringing.

The new round of questioning caught her off guard, and she was careful with her answers, sticking to the same story she had told the Void Knight investigators months earlier. Eventually, she understood they were only going through a practiced routine that wasn't specific to her. They didn't know her secrets, and she hadn't given them any reason to suspect there were any worth uncovering.

From there, she was sent to a team of hospitallers who subjected her to an impressively thorough physical examination. They collected a sample of everything from blood to spit and left no inch of her body unsearched. If she hadn't spent months in a medical bay being poked and prodded like unbaked bread, she might not have kept her cool.

Being immobilized and bedridden for weeks had a way of removing any sense of propriety or self-consciousness, at least when it came to one's body. She was only worried they would say she was unqualified due to her previous injuries. To get this far and fail because of something she couldn't change or control would break her.

The examination naturally led to a litany of questions about the injuries to her leg and hips. They questioned the impressively large scars and X-rays showing enough plates and screws to fill a mechanic's shop.

Through all of it, she insisted she was ready and able to serve. Even if the experience left her crippled or dead, she was committed now to see it through. The hospitaller in charge seemed unconvinced but simply muttered, "Where there's a will, there's a waiver," and signed off on her paperwork.

The experience culminated in a digital exam that spit out questions as quickly as she could answer them on every topic from Republic history to advanced mathematics. It wasn't her strength, but she did the best she could.

The results weren't divulged, but she must have done well enough to pass. In the end, she was given an ID card with her name and the position of "Applicant" on it. Included with the ID was a packet that provided basic information on where and when to arrive for the trials. She would have a little more than two months to prepare.

The whole screening process took nearly six hours and left her exhausted. If she had known what was in store when she got to Keplar, she would have taken a day to rest beforehand. At least it worked out and she had made it through the initial selection process.

Any thoughts of exploring the surface vanished with her energy, and she went straight back to the hotel. The Keplar staff helped arrange her transport and she arrived back without any incident.

Her room in the hotel was massive. It had not only a bed larger and softer than any she'd ever had but also a large seating area with its own desk, a private bathroom and even a kitchenette. The room was practically the size of their family apartment on Titan but with infinitely fewer bugs.

Arabella collapsed face first into the bed. The sheets smelled of flowers, and it was the softest thing she had ever felt, at least since she bought that floral-patterned fleece blanket from the Jovian trader in the dome.

The only thing that might be more luxurious was the large porcelain tub in the bathroom. It was like the ones she had seen in movies. Her stomach growled loudly. The quicker she found something to eat, the sooner she could come back and soak.

That was when she found the menu on the desk and realized she could order food directly. She didn't know what most of the items on the menu were, but she was excited to find out. She only wished her family could have been there to experience it with her.

CHAPTER
16

The two months that followed her initial visit to Keplar Industries went by quickly. She remained in the hotel with Namtar as her de facto guardian. Although at fifteen she was an adult, he filled the role of parental figure and tutor. Two things she had lost for good on Phoebe.

It turned out he knew a great many things about a multitude of subjects. From astronomy to warfare, he was well versed, and she wondered many times about his origins. He claimed adamantly that he was not a lord, but she didn't believe him. His breadth of knowledge and demeanor oozed sophistication and a privileged upbringing.

They trained nonstop, and it left little time for anything else. From lifting heavy weights to calisthenics, math, history, and even weapons fighting. The sights and sounds of Luna were forgotten in her efforts. All her focus went to the new mission of succeeding in the selection trials and nothing else. The hotel gym became the forge for her body. Its library became the hammer that shaped her mind.

It was impossible for her to make up for the years of education she missed while living on Titan, but two months was enough time to harden her body. However Namtar stressed she also needed a sharp mind. So he taught her tactics and logic, things that could be used to solve a multitude of problems.

The trials were always evolving, but Namtar said there would be a variety of challenges designed to evaluate her core abilities. Namely fortitude, problem solving, strength of arms, and leadership. There would be some who would lead, some who would follow, and others who wouldn't make it. It seemed ominous, but she figured he only wanted her to take it seriously.

They trained and trained until her body felt stronger than it had ever been in her life. She even felt competent enough to wield a ceramic blade or lightning pike without looking foolish. She felt as ready as she could be without knowing what was coming.

Arabella no longer worried her injured leg would snap from underneath her. She came to trust it again and in doing that started to trust herself. Namtar's training gave her purpose, and she relished it. The newfound strength filled her with pride, which emboldened her.

She was waiting at the hotel's landing port, a bag packed with her simple belongings. Namtar arrived soon after with his own things.

"I guess this is it," she said, moving her sunglasses on top of her head. Her eyes finally adjusted to the light, and she didn't have to squint furiously.

He nodded. "I must part ways with you here, but I'm impressed by the progress you've made in such a short time. You have a lot to learn, but with a strong foundation there's no limit to your growth."

"How will I find you again when this is all over?" She resisted the urge to cry. It would be unbecoming of her new persona.

"Fate will bring us together again, but not for a while, I think."

She knew he was right. When the trials concluded, she would be selected for entry to whichever school picked her. Then she would be expected to report for duty immediately. The choice would be out of her hands. "Maybe I could wait a while longer, try to get a spot in another recruiting class. It would give us more time to train."

He put a hand on her shoulder. "You're ready for this part."

She hoped he was right. "Thank you, Namtar. I owe you my life. If I can ever repay that debt, I will. I swear it."

He smiled. "And I swear to protect you with all my strength when fate sees fit to connect us again. Goodbye, Arabella."

She suddenly embraced him in a hug. "Don't say goodbye if you plan to see me again. It's only 'see you later.'"

He stiffened at first, but then slowly his muscles relaxed. He wrapped his free arm around her before pulling her away with a laugh. "Fate is a dog, always walking closely behind."

"Another old saying?" she said, fixing her hair, a smile glued to her lips. "Are you sure you aren't Armanic?" He always had baubles of wisdom that felt out of place or old-fashioned.

He nodded and with one final farewell boarded a waiting transport. She watched him go, thinking it was for the best he wasn't big on feelings. She didn't think she could have kept it together if he was.

The ride to the meeting spot for the start of the trials turned out to be quite long. They sped out along the surface until they were free of the city skyline and then bypassed several different cities. Eventually arriving at a relatively quiet-looking crater filled to the brim with water. On the edge of the lake was a large complex of buildings that were thoroughly nondescript.

The pilot touched down on the landing pad where a steady stream of ships came and went. There was everything from public transports like hers to private pleasure ships and large military vessels. Clusters of people stood near their vehicles, engaged in emotional goodbyes, and she passed by more than one parent providing an impassioned speech about faith and fortitude.

The parents were clergy men and women in elaborate robes, military officials in crisp uniforms, and all sorts of other well-dressed and otherwise important-looking figures. She threw away her misconception that she would be competing against other impoverished but talented youths. She would be up against the very best Luna could assemble.

Arabella weaved through the crowds, following signs that directed her toward the main entrance. She didn't dwell on the fact she was there alone, although she knew her mother would have hated all of it. Her father would have praised her immensely or perhaps been jealous that she would succeed where he had failed as a youth.

At the entrance was a snaking line of people waiting to enter. Everyone looked young, but she knew the ages varied anywhere from fourteen to the age cap of twenty-two, putting her on the younger end of the spectrum, although physically she was larger than most of the girls and even a fair number of the boys. She hoped it would be helpful.

Republican Guardsmen in blue burnished exoarmor stood as silent sentinels while uniformed soldiers processed the entrants. Up on a balcony was a cluster of other important-looking figures. They wore flowing robes and military uniforms festooned with medals and decorations. They were the ones they were all here to impress.

She was getting a fair number of stares as the line snaked back and forth through the ropes. In front of her were a pair of boys who looked almost identical, except for their haircuts. They both had dark-brown hair, but one had a short buzz cut and the other had long, shoulder-length locks.

They were speaking Armanic, but their skin was far less pale than hers, their accents more polished. Their eyes were darker too, a swirl of brown and gray.

She tried greeting them in her own, rough Armanic accent. "Any idea how long this line will take?"

The boys stopped their conversation, turning to look at her. "What crater did they pull you out of? Did you paint that on yourself?" the one said, motioning to her face.

The other said, "You sound like you fell out of a history book." They both laughed.

Brushing an invisible hair from her face, she flushed, unsure what to say. The line had backed up behind her, and it was hardly moving. She had nowhere to go. "I just moved here from Titan."

The long-haired boy's lips curled into a smirk. "You don't say. How'd a piece of driftwood like you end up here?" The line began to move. "You know what, I don't care. You won't be here long enough to remember."

The boy with the buzzcut added, "I'm surprised you were even able to write your own name on the forms. I hear most of you are illiterate out there." The twins had another good laugh.

The gap in front of her grew, a mix of anger and embarrassment locking her feet in place. She had only wanted to be friendly and quell her anxiety. Instead, it was amplified tenfold.

A girl behind her with black hair and light-beige skin said, in a Lunese accent, "Move it, ice rat."

When Arabella didn't budge, she repeated herself more slowly. "I said move it."

Another boy beside her on the other side of the snaking line said, "I don't know why they let the driftwood take a spot from local talent, not that they'll last long."

These people all seemed to have no problem badmouthing her right to her face. The soldiers in charge approached and more forcefully moved Arabella along. Eventually the heckling stopped when the line split off into smaller lanes.

Arabella rubbed her eyes aggressively and focused on the things Namtar taught her. She had to keep her temper and composure or all of this would end before it started. If she punched one or all of them in the face like she wanted to, the soldiers would drag her away. She would lose her chance to change things, probably forever.

She had been through worse. Would she really let some snotty, privileged brats break her? If it was that easy, what hope did she ever have of passing the trials or her schooling afterward.

Arabella brooded, stewing over the insults she had received since the moment she left the dome. Each one added to her growing list of personal slights and sense of otherness. Whether it was the Solites, the Armanic diaspora, or even the Armanics of the Far Coast. Each of them found some reason to dislike her.

She was always too much of a Solite because of her father's lineage or not enough because of her mother's Armanic heritage. Then she was either too rich and privileged from her life in the dome or not privileged enough for the brats she met here on Luna. Even the ones who were Armanic didn't value that over their Lunese heritage. The Far Coast was still a faraway place to them where people were basically mutants or drooling imbeciles. She hated being associated with it.

If she ever wanted to belong, she would need to fit in somewhere, embrace a new persona that wouldn't immediately disgust the people she met. Being Armanic was a liability, even if it was what she had always wanted since she was a little girl. She couldn't hide her Jeevan, but she could reject her Far Coast origins. Maybe that would be enough.

She reached the front of the line after what felt like an eternity. There a machine-like soldier scanned the ID card she received from Keplar. It was her entry ticket for the trials.

"Verify your name," he asked, looking up from the digiscreen.

She affected the best Lunese accent she could. "Arabella, Arabella Smith."

He scrunched his brow, "Current residence, Notus City, Titan?"

"No, sir, Pallas City, Luna." She needed a new beginning.

The soldier typed something into his device. "Right, sign here, here, and here. Then place your palm when it tells you," he said, indicating the digipad in front of her.

She placed her hand on the screen. There was a flash, followed by a green light. Then he waved her through and shouted. "Next!"

Julianna Serra had died in that dusty clerk's office on Titan, and in that moment on Luna, Arabella Smith was truly born.

CHAPTER

17

Arabella left her tale there. The rest was important certainly, but not for Mizraei to hear. She had already told him much more than he deserved. She ultimately found the exercise cathartic after keeping the story to herself for so long.

She didn't hate her mother anymore for what had happened. Arabella realized now that her mother was young and naive when she ran away to Titan. She made mistakes, but it was in service to what she thought was right. Even if it came with unintended consequences.

She never saw Namtar again. His training had been invaluable and his friendship even more so. Qilin was a man of his word in the end, but the trials were far from easy, and the events that followed tested her further. Without Namtar's intervention, she was confident she would never have gotten here.

"Well, did you like the tale?" Arabella said, placing the last stone on the board.

Mizraei smiled. "Yes, very much. I feel like I've waited a lifetime to hear the beginning. I never thought I'd live long enough to see how it ended."

Arabella snorted and drew her pistol. Her eyes glanced over the Go board. She had won, but it hardly felt fair against a nearly blind elder. "When did you realize who I was?"

"Then or now?" he said, his grin even wider. Surely, he knew why she was there, but somehow he was still jovial. "Well, this time I knew right away. Something always told me you would come back one day. No one else ever comes to see me anymore, not after everything that happened."

He took a particularly long puff of his nectar pipe. "I never believed Buckley when he said you died all those years ago, but I couldn't prove it. You did a good job hiding."

"I can thank Lady Vardan for that." She had the pistol pointed at him, but something stopped her from pulling the trigger. She had dreamed of this moment, imagined what it would be like to finally get her revenge, but something still gnawed at her. "How did you know who I was the first time? Was it the transport we sold you?"

Mizraei laughed. It was short and stunted like him. "Hardly. Stolen transports aren't that rare, and the bounty hadn't even been set yet. No, it was your friend Finn who tipped me off, and then I contacted Buckley to help collect you."

She lowered the gun slightly. "Finn? How would he have known anything?" She couldn't fathom how he was involved. He and Maggie had always been there to help her family from the very beginning.

"He never told you why I came to own this place, did he?"

"You made him an offer that was too good to pass up," she said, but the seed of doubt he planted was already sprouting.

"Then why is he still here?"

She didn't know. It surprised her to see him, but she thought he might not have come up with anywhere else to go. Maybe he preferred the familiar sight of the bar he once owned. Or he wasn't so proud and ambitious that he couldn't stomach someone else in charge.

"No need to answer. Your silence already has. He lost the bar to pay for his gambling debts."

She lowered the gun to rest on her thigh. The pieces weren't quite coming together. "What does any of that have to do with me?"

"Your family made a name for themselves completing so many deliveries for the Coalition. From what I heard, leadership wanted to cut out the middlemen and bring you into the fold more directly."

Arabella wasn't convinced. "We were already working for the Coalition. What did it matter who gave us the jobs? We were just another group of low district transporters. I still don't understand what this has to do with you or Finn's debt."

"I'm getting there," Mizraei said impatiently. "This is what I've learned through my own investigation, but it makes sense given the story you just told me. The Coalition higher-ups wanted to make sure you could be trusted with bigger jobs, so they started asking a lot of questions."

Arabella held her breath, fearing where his story would go.

"Finn told them what he knew, and they became even more insistent. That's why they left you that last job. A juicy morsel you wouldn't pass up to bring you closer into their web."

Mizraei coughed loudly, a wet hacking cough. She worried he might collapse before finishing his story. The guard opened the door to check on him, and she turned her body to hide the gun.

Mizraei waved the large man away as the cough subsided. When the guard was gone, he continued, "That last job came in after his wife had already left him. Poor timing really. Finn knew I had no love for the Coalition and offered me the information he had on you and that special shipment in exchange for his freedom. You see, his debt has him locked in my service until such a time as he pays it off."

He gestured with the pipe. "Anyway, at first I had no interest in the information because I knew Finn was an idiot. But then I wondered why the Coalition cared so much about some random ice rats. Why was it they wanted you and that brother of yours so badly? It took some digging, but through my contacts it was easy enough to put it all together given the timeline."

Arabella was stunned. Not because Mizraei claimed to have figured out a great mystery years ago, when she had already revealed it to him right now, but because all these years she had never considered Finn had been the one who ratted them out. He filled a special role in her heart after showing her that first kindness when she arrived on Titan. It didn't feel real that he would turn on her after being so selflessly kind.

Her mind worked through the events all those years ago to see where she had gone wrong with Finn. It would be a lot to unpack, but it would have to wait for a quieter time. It may have been out of ignorance, but if true it would make Finn as responsible as Mizraei for her family's death.

Arabella raised the gun back up. There wasn't anything else she needed to know. "It's a shame my uncles didn't pay much of a bounty for corpses.

You might have been able to live somewhere nicer than this shit hole. Happily ever after and all that. I guess my brother alone was only worth so much split however many ways," she sighed. "Goodbye, Mizraei."

A sickly wheeze escaped his lips, followed by a soft laugh. Arabella paused a second time in exacting her revenge. She wasn't sure if she could gather her nerves for a third attempt.

"Oh, you poor girl," he said, shaking his head. "It was your father who ordered it, even though he barely had a penny to his name. Your aunts and uncles wanted nothing to do with Armanic half-breeds, lest it sully their pure Imperial blood."

Her mind raced to process the implications of her father's survival. "And my... My brother, is he alive?"

"That's a rather sad story," he said somberly.

"Tell me, you cowardly sard." She waved the gun at him, but his milky eyes didn't register the threat.

"You see, your father never had a son. Yes, you did have a brother, but Oliver wasn't his. When he found that out, he refused to pay any bounty at all. We all got nothing. Except for that terrible stone in payment for your deaths. It's barely more than a trinket."

Arabella followed his eyes back to the pink stone he was staring at before. Now she knew why it looked so familiar. She stood up abruptly and stepped to the case. Up close it was easier to recognize. It had been a part of her father's gem collection. A piece he received from her and Mother as a gift on his birthday. It was the last birthday Arabella spent with him.

"What happened to my brother?"

She had assumed he was already dead from the injuries he sustained. There was little in his condition at the time that gave her hope he could have survived. They were in a remote part of the system, and what could one hospitaller in a lifeboat do to help?

For years following, she combed news from the Far Coast for any mention of him. The death or homecoming of a long-lost Serra would have certainly been reported on. The more time that went by without news, the more she accepted he had died. She did the math quickly in her head. He would be nearly twenty-seven. She couldn't imagine him as a grown man.

Mizraei kept talking through her silence. "Since Oliver wasn't his son, it made him a servant of his household. Your father quickly dismissed him from the position, and I offered him a new contract, housing and a job here with me."

"He was a child," she said through gritted teeth.

"It was all perfectly legal. He was an orphan and unconnected to any estate or business. Therefore, he was his own master," Mizraei said as if discussing importation taxes. What he described might be legal, but it still disgusted her.

Indentured servitude was far too common in the Far Coast and benefited only the wealthy. What other choice would a little boy have then to sign such a horrid contract? She wished she would have been surprised by her father's actions.

"Where is he?" she growled. Her revenge was almost forgotten. Now she longed for the prospect of seeing her brother, of having a family again.

Mizraei calmly took another puff of his pipe, considering his next words. "Not here, but I know where he is."

She rushed forward, pressing the cold steel of the gun barrel to his head. "Tell me. Now," she growled in a low whisper.

He flinched against the barrel, raising his arms in a shrug. "I don't know *exactly.*"

She draped her finger over the trigger. "Then you're of no more use to me."

"I'm ready to meet the creator, but I'd rather hear a few more stories before I do. I know where your brother went but haven't had news in a long time." Arabella pressed the gun harder. "Tommy Buckley, for reasons I can't fathom, paid three times his contract value to have him instead. Being a businessman, I couldn't refuse such a strong return on my investment. Last I heard, they were on Luna."

Luna... All this time, Oliver might have only been miles away. The reality tore at her fabricated armor, shattering it like so many shards of glass. She could have found him. She could still have a family.

"I can help you find him. I may be old, but I still have resources. I can-"

She cut him off. "My Jeevan was given to me for surviving. At the time, it made me feel brave because I was young and ignorant. Now my skin itches at the memory, a constant reminder of everyone I've lost and my many, many mistakes."

His cloudy eyes looked up at her. His voice was raspy and dripped of snake oil. He would tempt her with his poison fruit. "Let me help you. No one else knows what happened to him but me. You came here for answers, didn't you? I'm offering you that and more."

She snickered. "I'll explain in terms you can understand. You made a bad deal, and now the consequences have come due. You've never helped me before, and you aren't going to now. Only I can fix this, and right now I'm closer than I've ever been before. You aren't going to ruin that for me."

She pulled the trigger.

CHAPTER
18

Arabella's veins froze, and she squinted against the imagined cold. Time moved to a standstill, and suddenly she was back on the ice. A little girl again, huddled against the harsh winds, but they didn't welcome her this time. The ice, her birthright, still wasn't hers to claim, at least not yet.

She was born a child of two worlds but never at home in either, no matter how hard she tried to assimilate. The Jeevan marked her as ice born, but it was a painful lie. Hers was a tale only partially told. However, now she finally saw the faint light that would guide her through the blizzard. For the first time, she was able to step into the deep snow without fear of an endless crevasse.

Mizraei was guilty, and for that he had to die. It was hardly the first time she killed, but she wondered at how it made her feel. Violence was always appropriate in service to justice. It was one of the earliest lessons she ever learned. That she felt so unsettled confused her.

Her actions were in line with every known law of man from the Republic's Holy Scripture to the old Armanic Code. The guilty were supposed to suffer. The guilty were meant to die.

What she did only sped up the process that was already claiming his body. He was rotting from the inside, but Arabella wasn't going to let his foul and tainted presence ruin any more of her life. He received just payment for actions rendered. She would take the revenge she was owed before God, or nature could steal it from her.

The world snapped back into existence only a moment after the shot was fired. A shiver ran down her spine, but her eyes remained focused on exacting her vengeance.

She heard a rustling at the door and raised her pistol, quickly firing several more times through the thin door. She wasn't sure which guard she hit but heard a heavy thud as a body crumbled to the ground.

A moment later, the fat man burst through the door, rifle in hand. He must have picked it up from his fallen comrade. He fired blindly and untrained in long bursts into the room. Arabella dove aside as glass cabinets and wood splintered.

She returned fire, and he fell quickly, his body landing heavily on broken splinters of furniture and glass. These weren't trained soldiers. They weren't even competent street toughs.

This ponderous man had been there since the beginning. One of Mizraei's lackeys. A man without any honor. She remembered how he took pleasure in almost capturing her on Phoebe, leering in the shadows while Buckley did the dirty work. He was as guilty as the others for his role in furthering Mizraei's illicit dealings.

Arabella stood, dusting herself off. Looking back, she saw the pink gem her mother had given Father. The case unharmed by the gunfire.

She remembered helping her mother pick it out during one of the rare market days in the dome on Enceladus. It was a gift Arabella had been so proud of. Something she thought her father would like. It was bright and vibrant like her mother had been back then. In this place, it lost its luster like she had, like they all had.

Arabella moved to the case and shattered the cheap glass enclosure with the butt of her pistol. Reaching in through the shards, she pulled out the large gem and cradled it in her arm. Something so beautiful didn't belong in a place like this. She stepped through the shards of glass that crunched under her boots toward the door. She wouldn't spare the dead anymore of her time.

In the hallway, she found the last guard shambling toward her. He was holding his cudgel uncertainly, and she watched in the pregnant silence as he made his decision to live or die. His arm twitched as if to raise the club, and she unleashed her verdict, emptying the last rounds from her pistol. For the crime of being complicit, he likewise died.

The building was silent as she unleashed her wintery rage, and she was glad no one had been staying in the rooms above them. She was losing control, and she didn't think she could stop herself from harming anyone else who got in her way. Innocent or not.

She quickly changed the magazine of her pistol. Uranium-tipped bullets, suitable for armored targets and the wicked alike. When she entered the bar area, there was no one there to greet her but Finn. Whatever resources Mizraei claimed to still control was obviously a lie, as no one else came to help him.

Finn stood stiffly behind the bar, his hands held up and free of any weapons. She had trusted him, and he betrayed her. Sold a child off to a monster to cover for his own feebleness.

She approached him slowly. Her hand shook as she held the gun out toward him. His betrayal felt so much worse. "You sarding bastard, why? Tell me, you craven dog!"

"I... Bella, is that really you?" He looked on the verge of tears. "I regret what I did every day. Its why I never left here. Maggie never spoke to me again when she found out what I did. I deserve to be in this hell. It's what God wants for me."

"Why?" she croaked out. "You helped me, were kind to me, and then you fed me to the wolves."

Tears ran down his cheeks, and his voice cracked. "I thought you were some missing kid, a runaway from some magnate's estate. I always knew you were too smart, too polished. You didn't belong here Bella. I wanted to help you get home. Looking at you now, I know I made the right choice."

"You sarding prick. You sold me out to cover your own degeneracy. You're weak and pitiful."

He didn't try to deny it.

She stepped closer, the pistol shaking in her hand. The bar was the only thing separating them. "*You* don't get to decide where I belong. I'm Armanic like you."

Finn was the recipient of her words, but she wasn't yelling at him any longer. "This moon was my home, like the ice, but they were both taken from me, because of *you*."

She saw her father standing there in her mind, stoic and regal, the chains of nobility moving on his face. He was facing Imogen, her mother, a young girl, scared with two small children clinging to her sides. He offered none of them an apology. Imogen had wanted to leave, but he never let her go. When she finally had the courage to run, he sent these men to chase his own family like criminals.

Finn might have sensed she went somewhere else and began moving away snapping her out of her thoughts. "You stay right where you are."

Finn stopped and the door chimed, signaling the arrival of someone new. She repositioned herself to have an eye on Finn and the door. To her surprise, it was Henry.

Seeing the gun in her hand, he moved quickly inside, drawing a pistol of his own. "What's going on, Sergeant?" he said, keeping it professional like he always did around strangers.

"Some unfinished business. You can wait outside. I'm almost done," she said, keeping her eyes on Finn.

Finn said shakily, "You have it all wrong. I didn't do what you think I did. I'm a victim here. You already killed Mizraei. You got your revenge."

Henry moved past her into the hallway to clear the rest of the building. He came back a moment later, a blank expression on his face. "We can hand him over to the Watch on our way off world. You don't need to kill him."

"Yes, I do," she said quickly. "He sold me out once, and he'll do it again. I don't want my father to know I'm coming."

Henry looked surprised. "Your father? You said you had no living family."

"I thought I didn't, but it turns out I still might, at least for now." She thought her quest ended with Mizraei, but now it had just begun.

Finn tried to plead, his hands raised up to her and Henry. He reached for salvation. "I only ever tried to pay my debts. When I found out you were a Serra, I knew you didn't belong here."

Henry turned to her, his look of bewilderment obvious. She hated Finn even more now. Here, for a second time, he ruined her life by destroying the walls she was hiding behind. She tried to pull the trigger, but her finger wouldn't move.

Henry came in beside her and placed his bare hand on hers to lower the weapon. "This isn't what justice looks like."

She hesitated, her jaw clenched. This was exactly what justice was. It was what honor demanded. Surely, he could see that. She resisted, keeping the gun trained on Finn.

Henry continued, "I don't know your tale, but killing him won't bring anyone back. It won't erase your pain. Killing will never add to your life. I know you know that."

She had killed so many times, the first time not far from here on Titan. Then dozens of times after, first in defense of her family and later in service to the Republic. He was right that none of it had improved her life, but that didn't make it less necessary for her survival. She didn't kill because she wanted to but because she had to.

From the day her family died, she stopped dreaming of what life could be. Revenge and survival were the only things they left her with, but sarding hell she knew he was right. Her heart ached for the girl she used to be before all of this happened. She began to lower her weapon.

It was in that moment of weakness that Finn reached below the counter for an old-fashioned shotgun. It was some antique from centuries past. He raised it as if to shoot them but was far too slow.

Henry fired several shots before he even had the weapon cocked. Arabella's own shots close behind. She thought she would be happy to see the life leave Finn's eyes, but there was only a tremendous sadness.

The room was quiet again, except for their steady breathing. They holstered their weapons, and Arabella walked to the bar, placing the pink gem down on the counter, before walking behind the bar.

She stepped past Finn's bleeding body and fetched a bottle of whisky she knew he kept behind the bar. Coming back to where Henry was standing, she set down two glasses.

Henry took a seat on a stool, and she sat next to him. They both stared forward at the mirrored surface and the collection of bottles behind the bar. She looked at his reflection in the mirror beside her own. Her pale skin and his sun-kissed cheeks.

His face betrayed his noble upbringing, but something dark was still hidden behind his gentle eyes. Whatever it was, it wouldn't be bad enough to bridge the gap between them. He deserved far better than her. He still had a chance to have that comfortable life his birth promised him.

"You should go with the others and leave me to deal with this," she finally said, breaking the silence. She would deal with the consequences of her actions.

"I'm not doing that."

"Because I'm a Serra? You should know my father is far from a favored son. He's taken more from the name than he ever added to it." She took a shot of the harsh liquid and then poured another.

Henry joined her. "I always suspected you were more than you said, but that doesn't matter. I'm here for you, nothing else. You saved me once, and I'm here to return the favor."

She said sarcastically, "Then you've done your honorable duty. You can leave now the noble knight and continue to save the solar system from tyranny. I'll only bring you more trouble."

"You have only ever done the opposite for me. From the moment we met you've supported me."

"I was doing my job."

He shook his head. "I don't think that's it. You want something more, like the rest of us."

"I stopped dreaming of the future a long time ago. When I thought my family was gone, and I was all alone, I swore I would never love or laugh again. I knew if I did, I would lose the source of my joy. I've been one breath away from the end ever since. Happiness isn't something I'm allowed to have," she said, looking away as tears began to well in her eyes.

Henry turned to look at her. "You aren't the only one raised in a living hell. You've seen my scars. My father wouldn't tolerate any sign of weakness, despite having an abundance of his own. Maybe beating them out of me was his way of addressing his own."

She had assumed his story was something along those lines, but to hear it said out loud threatened to break her. A child shouldn't have to endure such torment. "You seem to have thrived in spite of him."

Henry finished a second shot of whisky and poured themselves both a third. "No thanks to him. My mother died too young to temper his foul disposition, but my grandmother was an angel of a woman. She helped for a time."

Arabella wanted to hear his story, the tale told by his scars.

He went on, "When she died, all I had left to believe in was hope for a better future, until eventually I lost sight of even that in the darkness. One day I woke up and saw I was where you are now. Each day like the last through a terrible grind of routine and expectation."

"You're speaking like it isn't that way any longer," she said softly. She was afraid to hint at her longing for his encouragement but turned to match his gaze anyway.

He smiled reassuringly. "The day I met you on Mars, everything changed for me. Your support made it possible for me to believe in that future again, to believe things could be different for all of us. You risked everything to join me on this seemingly hopeless crusade."

"You made that decision on your own. I had nothing to lose, so I followed. It wasn't heroic." Her words were cold and lifeless.

"When I bore my punishment and escaped from the darkness, you were the one there to guide me. You've stayed by my side ever since, when you could have easily left or ratted me out to your own benefit. You're here because we both share the same dream," he said emphatically.

He turned fully now to pull her in close. She didn't resist his touch because it was everything. She buried her head into his shoulder as he spoke. "Even on the ice, there is spring and summer. That whisper of warmth on the horizon that signals you're still alive, that you made it through. This may be the darkest winter of your life, but spring always comes."

"You are my spring," she whispered into his ear.

"Then let me warm your heart, like you've warmed mine," he whispered back, and the world around them blurred.

"I can do this myself. I *should* do this myself."

He didn't pull back. "I have no intention of letting you walk alone."

Her resolve was weakening. "I'll hurt you, like everyone else. You deserve better."

He held her face and looked into her eyes. "I'm no stranger to pain. Even the thickest ice melts in the sunlight, so stop being so stubborn and walk with me."

She let out a small laugh and pressed her lips against his. It felt like the first joy she had expressed in a lifetime. She wanted to proclaim her love for him, but that was still a step too far. For now, his warmth would have to be enough.

After a time, he pulled away. "We should get to the others before anyone stumbles in here."

She stood up with a heavy sigh. She looked around the bar one more time. "I used to think this would be the end of my story, but maybe you're right. There's more to my tale."

"I'm sure there is, and I look forward to unraveling the rest of the story. I have no doubt it will be a tale worthy of telling. I know that means a lot to your people," Henry said.

She appreciated that, even if she still didn't quite believe him. "I've never known who my people really are, but I want to find out." She looked behind the bar at Finn's body and shook her head. "I wish he would have found that bravery years ago."

Henry nodded. "I'm not sure what his plan was."

"I think this might have been his plan. He was too much of a coward to pull the trigger himself," she said coldly. "I'm not sure if his wife is still around Titan, but we should look for her. She was a Coalition operative and could be useful."

Henry stood, adjusting his uniform. "Lead the way, Sergeant."

She picked up the large gem, cradling it in the crook of her arm, and smiled before heading for the door.

THE END